# HEROES
# THROUGH THE DAY

by

## RUEL WHITE

*Jaclie*

*Nie.*

*Ruel.*

LONDON ● PORT OF SPAIN

First published 1990
by New Beacon Books Ltd.,
76 Stroud Green Road, London N4 3EN, England

© 1990  Ruel White

ISBN: 0 901241 91 1  (hardback)
ISBN: 0 901241 92 X (paperback)

British Library data is available on request from the library.

Typesetting by An Grianán, 62bis rue de Vic, 62100 Calais, France
Printed by Villiers Publications Ltd., 26a Shepherds Hill,
London N6 5AH

I'm talking about making out the other side.
I'm talking about maintaining the sleeping, waking,
sleeping, waking cycle.
I'm talking about survival.
I'm talking about making it through the day.
Cling to those little dreams,
forever planning little schemes.
Hey! Living in make-believe is the only way out of here.
Got to get out of here.
Sometimes someone breaks through
and it gives a small boost to like me and you.
Hey! It could happen to me too,
you think.
One day I might get my wings and fly right on out of here.
But until then
let's just get through the day,
okay.
Boy, you should know the hassles.
They come from all sides.
Coming up from under.
Coming down.
In a dance.
In your house.
Drinking.
Just making out.
But it's okay,
'cos there's always something that comes along
which helps.
And yeah,
everything's better in LA.

# The Wall

## 1

Butch and Derrick are leaning against the wall outside *The Hope*. Joanne's with them. Her friend went off with some guy, telling her to wait 'cos she'd only be a short while. So she's waiting for a friend and it's three o'clock in the afternoon on a Monday. She's dressed to kill in her party trouser-suit; the sky blue, glittery one; like something out of Dallas; a creation fit for the Dynasty Dolls; like something Sue-Ellen or Krystle would wear; quarter-back shoulders and all. Only thing is, it looks as if she's had it on for a couple of days, or worn it out the night before — which of course she had. Her aunt said it made her eye catching, so she wore it frequently.

It's a hot day.

*The Hope* stands on the corner of a street leading to a main road. The main road hasn't got any of the big supermarkets or many attractive shops, so it isn't very busy. There's another high street close by, where you can find all the chain stores and stuff. You know, stuff like Macdonalds, Ravels, cinemas, pubs for drinkers, gang fights and egged on ('Use it. Use it. He's asked for it. Here, give it to me. If you haven't got the bottle, I'll do it') stabbings. It's not that great during the week but Fridays and Saturdays are the worst. On weekends only the young, confident or well sussed go down there.

The main road on which *The Hope* stands is pretty narrow. When there isn't a lot of traffic about, you often see friends hail one another from opposing pavements. They may even hold a neat little conversation, like —

'Hey, long time no see. Where've you been hiding yourself?'
'Well I'm getting on a bit now so I'm settling. How about you?'
'No man. You with a damsel?'
'Yes.'
'The same one you've got the youth with?'
'Well, it couldn't be anyone else really.'
'It's a boy you've got, isn't it?'
'Two of them.'
'Two boys. You're doing well. So you don't rave at all now?'
'No. I've had to give all of that up.'
'You're under manners then?'
'No. Pressure.'
And they laugh.
'Look, I've got to get back to work . . .'
And a lorry zooms by.
'I didn't catch that.'
'I've got to hurry, but check me.'
'Are you still living at the same place?'
'In a way. Same block but the flat above. Directly above where I used to live.'
'Got it. Later.'
'Later.'

— before carrying on about their business. This happens around *The Hope* all the time and it's nice, but when two people who aren't at peace meet it's not so nice. It's frightening to those appreciative of fear.

*He waits in the courtyard by the stables at midday on Sunday. And the church bell chimes twelve times. He takes the butt from his lips, flings it on the ground and grinds it in the dirt with his Cuban heel.*
*Four figures come into view. The bells chime with each step they take. The figures change from vague outlines to solid, clear shapes. They stop and the bell stops.*

Joanne told Butcher and Derrick that she'd be in LA in two weeks time. She'd be out there for three weeks and come back — to sort out a little business — then go out to stay.

One time Butch made a lot of money. He was getting it direct from a friend he went to school with. His friend thought of himself as The Man. The Man was called Julius Constantine Isaacs because his father wanted him to be a great leader. The Man was smart, he made one big killing and shift; split back home. Now he sends it over. No big thing, just a small operation. Existing, you know. More a small wholesaler than manufacturer stroke supplier to the trade. (If to say manufacturer is right here.) Let's say The Man's a cultivator and went to school in this country with Butch and D.

Derrick was a year younger than Butch and The Man, so whilst at school he never knew them very well. They were only faces to him. They got talking when they were sixteen, seventeen and met constantly at the same clubs and boogie dance. Derrick dressed smart when he went out and he was tall. He looked smooth and deadly. They started calling him Big D when he was in earshot and Peanut when he wasn't. The first words D ever said to Butch and The Man were, 'I'm not a youth, you know.' Don't mess, he meant. So, Butch and The Man immediately acted cool with D. The Man started calling him by his name instead of Youth as he had before. Derrick ignored him, whatever handle he used. D didn't dig The Man at all, thought him too stand-offish, big-headed, aiming for a big come down. 'Let him try and come clever with me,' thought Derrick. But he'd always liked Butch, so they were cool to one another straight away.

Even in the midst of a sea of sinking, drowning, dying bodies (mere flesh) the great man Julius saw himself floating safely, treading o'er the water Jesus-like, back to Terra Firma (mother earth).

Derrick felt confident in his ability to deal with The Man physically or mentally. With a man like The Man you have to get in first. You have to keep your guard up all the time. Like Muhammed Ali when he fought George Foreman; keep your guard up and wait. When Butch and The Man fell out D wasn't too upset. They fell out over a deal. I think The Man only sent Butch two lots. Butch considered the second batch short. It was still over a weight but short nonetheless.

Short on what he'd got the first time and short on what he'd expected. Butch sneaked into the office where he worked and made an international call to The Man to reason things out.

The Man didn't want to talk and slammed the phone down. He was at his uncle's bakery. He told his uncle to tell Butch to fuck off if he rang back.

'You youths want to behave. The trouble with you is you don't know how to conduct yourselves properly,' his uncle replied. 'You love to chat as if you're the only person that knows anything about business.' He concluded contemptuously, 'Now fuck off, English boy.'

The Man stood rigid in the bakery door. Shocked. His uncle had seen him burp after supping at the breast, struggle to sit up, shit in his nappies until two and a half and bawl like hell when told off for being a naughty boy. 'Go on. Just fuck off. You're nothing here. You think you're some kind of film star.'

So much for mother earth. So much for the security of terra firma. But Butch didn't ring back. He left the job before he got sussed about the phone call. He had another angle anyway.

He sold what he had and spent the money capping two teeth in gold, so that everyone would know he'd made some money, once. But that's Butch for you, drawn to things which glitter.

*The Hope* is a public house and the public have it. There is a brick wall about four feet high separating the street from the yard. It inspires images of Norman castles with moats around them for defence. The yard made you think of a moat.

Tommy Boy and his crew drew up in their BMW. He stuck his head out of the wound-down window and smiled. Paul wound down the window at the back, stuck his head out and smiled too. Hangman and Soulboy were in the car with them. They were looking at the trio and smiling. They say that Hangers killed a man once and got away with it, and that's what's turned him so bad. His name is Simon Dubois. He was in the same class as Butch all through school.

The trio were staring back. D turned from looking at the car and spat on the ground, then turned and looked at the car again with a hardman's expression. He looked at Butch, then at Joanne, then the car again and spat on the floor a second time. He sucked his teeth. Hangman was out of the car and striding up to them in an instant. 'What have you done?' Butch muttered.

'Leave it,' yelled T Boy from the car. 'He's a boy. A little fucking baby.' Hangman was standing right up to Derrick. Of about equal height and build, they stood face to face, eye to eye, nostrils together, flaring, sharing breath and almost kissing. Joanne and Butch back away slightly.

— If she screams, she's dead. If he intervenes, the others will look upon it as an invitation to do their bit. And so, like diners at one of those restaurants where couples make it on sheets of perspex hanging from the ceiling above the tables, they watch an intimate moment. —

Hangman had his cane with him. The one with the concealed sword. He pulled the cane's handle, slowly revealing, bit by bit, the glint of a sheer metal. He'd give D sight of an inch or so and sheath it, then start pulling it out another time.

'Hey, Butch, got any wheels yet?' That was Soulboy, calling from the car.

Ignoring Souls, Butch tries to talk to Hangers, 'He's young, man. He doesn't want any trouble with you. You guys are in a different league.'

In the car, Soulboy, Tommy and Paul passed smiles around. 'Just goes to prove, nobody's completely stupid,' Souls said, giving Paul a massive grin.

Hangman gave Butch a view of the steel and asked him if he wanted some.

'We were in the same class at school. I've known you too long for that.'

'Then shut your mouth.'

'Come off it.' Butch suddenly fell to the floor.

'Didn't I ask you something?' It was Soulboy, up behind him, looking around casually. His posture and manner as that of the cigar-chewing, poncho-clad, stubble-chinned gunslinger out of the spaghetti's, but sweeter. Soulboy is sweet.

'What?'

'Wheels? Have you got wheels?'

'No. I haven't got any.'

'That's better.' Soulboy produced a neatly-folded hanky from his back pocket, wiped his hands, drew it up to his nose and took in the aroma of the perfume he'd sprayed on it. He touched Hangman on the shoulder and said, 'Let's go.'

'Come on, Hangers,' yelled Tommy. 'We haven't got time to waste on these scavengers.' Upon mention of the word, scavengers, Paul — who was still in the back seat — crumpled up laughing. His laughter was infectious. He imitated T Boy again and again. 'Scavengers,' he'd say and start laughing. Soon Soulboy and Hangman were laughing too. 'I didn't know you knew any words with more than four letters?' Soulboy shouted back at T. Paul said the word again, pointing at Joanne and Butch and Derrick. He was really rolling up now.

Souls started back to the car, he turned to Hangman, 'Coming?' Hangman said, 'Next time I'm going to kill you,' to Derrick before heading back to the car, behind Soulboy.

Tommy Boy started up and drove the gang away.

'I could have taken him.'

'They're rubbish, Del. Don't get down to their level, they're not worth it,' Joanne advised.

'Go and call them back, Big Man, if you want to get yourself killed,' Butch says and kisses his teeth as he slides down the wall until backside meets earth.

'I could have taken them.'

Joanne joins Butch, sitting by the wall, 'There's no need to prove yourself to them, Del.'

In the distance, a shape. That unmistakable gait. A bit of a slip in the dip and far too much slide in that glide. What's new today? Biggre, the soul of unpredictability and yet keeper of that constant flame, morality. Biggre, all things in one.

'Hey, Butch.'

'What?'

'I think this is a bad spot.'

'What do you mean?'

'Look,' Derrick pointed at Biggre.

'Oh no!'

'If it's bad news for you, what do you think it is for me? One minute I'm the finest thing on two pins and he wants to take me back to Africa, the next minute I'm the world's biggest whore.'

Quietly, Butch asked, 'Are you still his woman?' to rib and provoke her and prompt the usual round of denials, with too many explanations for what should be a simple yes or no, so there must be some truth in it.

'I met him round Sharon's. Once and only once. He was round there visiting his little boy while her boyfriend was out. Damon's really cute. They started arguing and Sharon stormed out. She was going mad. One minute they were talking, like we are now, next minute it was as if a bomb had exploded. Sharon was really having a go. Anyway, she shouts to Biggre, "Put him to bed, then get out. I don't want to see you here when I get back" and flounced off. She slammed the door so hard it nearly came off its hinges.'

Before she could finish, Biggre The Flame was upon them.

Furnished in robes of red, green and gold. A leather satchel hanging from a shoulder. He wore trainers. Black trainers. He had bells strapped to his legs by thongs dangling at his ankles, giggling, playfully sparkling, set against his black running shoes. Lots of bells. Silver and gold. There was a bell at the end of the bobble on his woolly hat. The bobble dangled at his middle back, chiming. His hair foamed at the fringe of his hat.

Magician like he spirits a wooden flute from the satchel and looks up into the tree in the garden next door to the pub. He blows two slow notes, one low the other high, then a little cluster, then nothing but he still holds the flute to his lips. A bird cheeps and he takes the flute away. Biggre looked at them, 'Even the birds know,' and walked on.

Joanne breathed a sigh of relief for the whole world to hear.

'So maybe you're not his woman after all,' said Butch.

'I've always said that.'

'Woman. Know thyself, like the birds.' The booming voice came out of the blue. 'It is not good for a woman to sit on the earth as a man. Your pussy will get germs.'

'I thought about warning you but I didn't want to bring you down,' Derrick interjected quickly before Biggre got into his stride. 'He's getting tricky in his old age.'

'Remind me never to use you as a lookout,' Butch replied.

'He was walking away from us, I blinked, and there he was charging back up here full steam ahead. And I'm going to be the best eyes you've ever had.'

Biggre the unstoppable and irrepressible. He pointed at Joanne and yelled, 'Jezebel,' with his lungs expanded to their fullest.

If the charge of Jezebel were seen as a straw, it would be that which broke Joanne the camel's back. She leapt to her feet and steamed up to Biggre.

Butch attempted to hold her but she was too quick. 'Do I need this?' he asked himself.

'Hope is a jinx,' swore Derrick.

'You're just as bad.'

'Hangman's nothing. One day I'll take his piece and ram with it.'

'You scare me,' and Butch feigned fear, then added mockingly, 'How will you do it? Just walk up to him and say excuse me, Mr Hangman, could I please have your sword, so that I may disembowel you? Or will you do your karate on him? Like Bruce Lee, as he slashes you, trap the blade between two fingers and disarm him at blistering speed. Bend him to your will using the secrets of the old masters. Then gut him.'

'I'll look after my business, you look after yours.' Derrick, Clint Eastwood style.

'Yeah Big Man. Get off your horse and drink your milk.'

'Shut up. If your woman doesn't watch it, Biggre's going to lay one on her.'

'What woman?'

'Look.' Derrick pointed at Jo facing up to Biggre. Screwing him up and down and chatting bad.

'She's not my woman,' Butch stated. 'Cut it out, Joanne,' he shouted. His head, almost with a life of its own, bobbles this way and that, from conversation to conversation. Like a boxer on the receiving end, trapped in a corner with his guard down.

'Don't you think you ought to go and break it up?' D asked casually, pointing and throwing a glance at the fighters.

'It's none of my business and cool it on the connections.'

'What's the connection, Butch?'

'You know her as well as I do. Do I call her your woman? No! So cool it!'

'She's off again.'

'Joanne! I said cool it.' Joanne carried on, disregarding Butch's diplomatic efforts. 'Let's go and break it up, D.'

'That's what I said, Butch.' As they started to Joanne and Biggre, Derrick again asked, 'What's the connection?'

'Fuck all, Derrick. Fuck all.'

Butch grabbed Biggre's arm as it fell towards Joanne's jaw. Biggre pulled his arm free and took two paces back from the trio.

'Joanne!'

'What, Derrick?' she answered, her eyes fixed firmly on The Flame.

'If you want your jaw broken, stay where you are. If you don't, come with us. Coming, Butch? We've broken it up.' Derrick started walking back to the wall.

'I just want to know why he keeps telling people I'm his woman. I've never been out with him.'

Derrick stopped in his tracks.

'Dirty liar. Jezebel,' Biggre replied.

Derrick turned back round. 'Don't say you weren't warned if he mashes you up, Joanne.'

'Mash who?' she got cocky.

'Whore.' Biggre yelled and raised his hand.

Joanne took two paces forward and set herself up nicely for full receipt of Biggre's thunderbolt.

'Hit me then,' she said defiantly.

'Hit you? I wouldn't piss on you.'

'You want my pussy though, don't you?'

Biggre kicked her in the stomach. 'I wouldn't soil my hands on you,' he spat, like a crazed or frightened cat.

D shoved Biggre's shoulder. 'There's no need for that.'

Biggre shoved him back. 'Move, Boy.'

D shoved him again. 'Try me?'

Butch pulled Derrick back. D wasn't expecting it. He tripped over his own feet, stumbled and fell on his arse. A day of constant backing down filled him with frustration. Everyone's pushing him. The day's cup of twenty-four hours overflowed with humiliation. People call him Big D. He sprang to his feet, grabbed Butch by the collar and hauled him up close. Butch hung from his hands like a rag doll, powerless and

10

floppy. Joanne screamed, 'Stop it!' And the red, green and gold Rasputin philosophically summised, 'The devil is between you.'

In unison, Butch and Derrick replied, 'Fuck off.' Derrick then freed his friend. Neither Biggre nor Joanne heard Butch quietly whisper in Derrick's ear, 'In real life Clint Eastwood would've died long ago. Life isn't a movie.'

'I know that. Do you?'

'We shall see. We shall see.'

Biggre disappeared in a puff of smoke.

Our heroes trudged, like battle-weary soldiers, back to the wall.

'It must be the heat,' one of them commented.


# 4


Derrick told Butch that he was going home.

'Wait a minute, I'll come with you,' he replied.

'Three's a crowd,' Derrick made a motion.

'Alright then,' Butch says then pauses slightly. 'Catch you later, Joanne.' He got up and prepared to walk off with Derrick.

'I'll see you when I get back,' she tried to shout but she was right choked, so her words came up through her throat bubbly because of the saliva that came up too. Her voice cracked before she'd completed the short sentence. It had all but vanished by the last word.

Butch stroked his chin, appeared puzzled and asked, 'Where are you going?'

'LA. I told you I'm off to LA tomorrow.'

Derrick whispered in Butch's ear. 'She's telling porky pies. Earlier she said she was leaving in two weeks.'

Ignoring his partner's comment he wished Joanne good luck, adding, 'You can't get any worse than here.'

'I know,' she said.

'Don't encourage her. Let's go man,' Derrick insisted. He put a heavy accent on go. Like, LET'S GO NOW. IMMEDIATELY!

'Oh. What am I talking about? I'm leaving in two weeks,' she added quickly and quietly. Derrick's eyes nearly popped out of their sockets. His mouth opened wide with astonishment and immense disbelief.

She got loud and excitable. 'It seems as if a whole month's wooshed by since we've been sitting here. Think of it, LA, where it all happens,' wistful. She asked Butch which way he was going.

'Around,' Derrick replied. He whispered in Butch's ear, 'Let's get away from here, Butch. All the people around here are mad. You can get a nutter anywhere. We've got choice. Let's go pick someone fresh. Some variety, at least.'

'She's not mad she's compulsive,' Butch said in defence of Joanne's state of mind.

'Compulsive, my arse.'

'How is she compulsive? Explain it to me, Brains.'

'I'm off.' Derrick stepped.

'Be round about nine.'

'Are we still going to do it?'

'Yes.'

'I don't know about this, Butch.'

'It's a cert.'

'Let me be straight.'

'Be straight, Derrick.'

'Have you got the bottle?'

'Have you? I'm a veteran.'

12

'I think so. It's all set up?'

'Of course. See you later. You're in with the big boys now.'

'Butch, don't be so flash.'

'Flash? Doesn't everyone want to go to LA?'

Butch offered Joanne his hand, which she took, and helped her to her feet. He then put his hand over her shoulder and walked off in the opposite direction to Derrick.

D shouted after him, 'Are you sure, Butch?'

'See you at nine,' Butch shouted back.

# The Penthouse

## 5

Butch is hard to pin down. If to try and try again will eventually result in success, how come Butch isn't successful? He tries hard enough.

'Where are you staying now?' she asked.

'I've got a place on *The Estate*.'

'Weren't you staying with Derrick?'

'That's ages ago. I couldn't stay there forever.'

'How did you get this place?'

'Through a friend.'

'What! Did they leave it for you?'

'You could say that.' He bent over and turned up the hem of a trouser leg which had fallen down. Neither of the legs were fastened. They delighted in falling alternately, never together, so when it wasn't one it was the other. He had a thin neck which floated inside his shirt collar; shirt collar done right up to the very top button. His clothes, shoes apart, looked too big. They probably weren't, but Butch's figure made you think they were. (Like an illusion. Like seeing what you want to see.) He was always this way since Joanne first knew him. But always clean. He was always clean. He'd never been done for anything either; never been caught. His parents have split up and he's got to look out for himself. But then again even when they were together and Butch was in his early teens and still at school, his classmates knew he had to wash his own clothes, cook his own meals and stuff. So it would be fair to say that Butch has always fended for himself. Boys being boys though, he drew the line at ironing, cooking anything too elaborate; in general, doing anything that could possibly be perceived as being too womanish.

His parents parting of ways didn't outwardly appear to have any effect on him. He never lost weight or became disinterested in things he enjoyed before the split. Always, the same old Butch. The gold teeth have never quite had the desired effect. His big problem was somewhere to live; not short-term. He knows how to doss and cadge floor space or from time to time get a woman with a place of her own. He dreamt of having his own place, of being in control for a while. A base from where he could plan and prepare himself for the next movement. A little bit of time to work out where to go from here. The Herbsman life was cool but it wasn't straight. It was high risk. Too high to claim having complete control over it. And dealing with people like Julius 'The Man' Constantine (his dad wanted him to be a great leader) Isaacs, was something he could well do without. He'd kicked himself loads of times since the phone call for not listening to Derrick's advice.

If Hangman, T Boy or any of the others were alone, Derrick would mess them up. One on one, armed or not, Derrick could handle any of them. But four on one, that's murder, and it would be! Because those boys are bad.

He got up from fixing his hem and asked, 'So what is it with you and Biggre?'

'You wouldn't believe me,' Joanne answered.

'I haven't said I don't believe you so far, have I?'

'You think you're smart, Butch. You just want a laugh.'

'Am I laughing? Have I laughed so far?'

'Biggre's mad.'

'Aren't we all?'

'Maybe. But we don't all hassle. Biggre hassles.'

'Not really,' he replied provocatively and she punches him lightly and playfully. 'I've got to be honest. If there were fifty people outside the pub today and Biggre felt like playing up, you'd be the one collecting. Guaranteed. Let's be fair, he is very partial to you, isn't he?'

16

'Alright then, I'll tell you. Remember his ex, Sharon, left me, him and the baby in the flat together. Sharon had a go at him and stormed out.'

'Yes. Hold on a second.' They stopped outside a newsagents. Butch went in and reappeared with cigarettes and papers.

'Got herbs?' she asked.

'No.'

'Hash?'

'No. So what happened?'

She shrugged her shoulders, puzzled.

'What happened at Sharon's after she left?'

'I didn't know you knew Sharon.'

'I don't.'

'Oh. It sounded as if you did. Anyway he went into Damon's room. Damon's their little boy. He's got a sort of box-room for a bedroom but it's done up real nice. He's really cute, got little dreadlocks and everything, really into music. Sharon's boyfriend's really into music. Whenever you'd go round there he'd be showing Damon something. Her fellah knows Redemption Song, you know, the Bob Marley record. He plays it on one of those guitars you don't have to plug in. He's a professional, always out rehearsing or playing. He's even been to studios. Now and again he goes on tour. I've known him to be away as long as six months touring. I'm forever babysitting for her. Don't get me wrong though, I love it. And Sharon needs the break. She's got a life too. It'd be unhealthy for her to be stuck indoors day in day out. It'd be soul destroying. Anyway, Damon's a lovely boy.'

'Where are you going?' he interjected smoothly.

'Nowhere special.'

'This way then.' And they turned left. 'Go on,' he instructed.

'You're acting strange all of a sudden, Butch.'

'Go on,' and he shook her slightly.

'Why so tense?'

'I'm not tense. Go on,' he again said, but this time with an overtly courteous tone and smiling at her.

17

'That's better,' and she shook him back and gave him a wry smile. 'Where was I?'

'Biggre's in Damon's room. And I know Damon's really cute and clever. Sharon's bloke is Bob Marley reincarnated and you should take up social work. Take it from Biggre in the baby's room and try not to digress, please.'

'Mr Ackerman!'

'Remember him?'

'Never forget. Funny how little silly things stick in the mind, isn't it? I mean, I can picture him right now —

Standing at the head of the class, facing us from between his desk and the blackboard; arms folded across his chest; churning the chalk between his fingers; every now and again stroking his chin with chalked hands, leaving streaks of pastel yellow, blue or misty white. A strange creature, misplaced in time. Like something from a bygone age, bifocals and all.

— I don't know why but every time I heard him tell someone not to digress, I'd want to roll up. What's so funny about the word digress. It must've been the way he said it or something.'

They walked through an arch into a courtyard.

'Home,' he said.

Home: four redbrick blocks encircling an unkempt lawn. The lawn is littered with discarded boxes, in bits; discarded cans of drink, half drunk; discarded bits of paper disclosing snatches of correspondence; bits of this and bits of that; bits. There was a second arch on the opposite side of the courtyard. This arch faced a third one and between the two were gardens, for ground floor residents. The third arch led you to a second courtyard surrounded by another four blocks. It's like the courtyard our heroes are in. *The Estate* is three such blocks of four, set out in a triangle. It's like a honeycomb, which might not be a bad analogy, especially when the place is buzzing.

The paladins are full, so people have had to leave black plastic

18

bags of rubbish around the huge bin's enclosure. Scavenging cats and dogs have slashed the bags open. As a consequence, you've got all the maggots and flies and slugs and stuff that hang around unattended filth. There is however one thing that must be said: there is never any trouble on the blocks. *The Estate* has a good reputation. There's a waiting list. A lot of families are crying out for a ground floor flat here.

A canal runs alongside *The Estate*. Beyond the canal is the park. So from one side you could see only greenery from the window. You could see all the animals scampering about in their pens. The park keeps chickens, goats, a pig and sheep. Beyond the park — and you can only just make it out — is the town hall. The town hall initially — to a tourist — seems some way away. But when you're here permanently, the distance becomes nothing. A stroll through the park on a summer's day. Fun snowball fights in winter. The park is big. One of the biggest. There are some well-kept houses in the streets around the back.

Yet it's on the main road, two minutes walk away, round the other side, where all the trouble happens. You know, The Badfightmainroad. There are people in dire straits, in desperate circumstances, unable to reason through pressing need, living in the area. Excitement and bustle isn't confined to the night-time. Jobs aren't easy to come by, so many people are on the street all the time, trying to live and stay upful. Trying to be positive. It's a constant battle. Who wants to simply exist? Choose life.

Joanne would never understand Biggre the way Butch did. (When nobody wants to listen and you have to shout and shout and shout to be heard, or at least that's the way it feels.)

'Where's home?' she asked, incidentally looking around at the top floors of the four intimidating buildings.

'Fourth floor. The flat right at the top. In the corner. Over there,' he pointed at it. 'The Penthouse Suite.'

'Where else?' she contributed. 'How do we get to the lift?'

'Lift?' He laughed.
'The exercise'll do me good. Lead the way, Chris.'
'Chris?'
'Bonnington.'
'Chris Bonnington?'
'The mountaineer.'
'Oh, I get it. What's a mountaineer?'
'Shut up.'

## 6

Butch tapped at the piece of cardboard covering the hole beside the lock. He put his hand through, jiggled around momentarily, then a sharp twist of his wrist and the door was opened.
'Didn't the people who left you the flat give you a key?'
'Not yet.'
'Who are your friends, Butch?'
'The people.'
'Terrific!'
He flicked a single switch and the entire flat at once became illuminated. Wide eyed, she pronounced, 'It's beautiful.'
'Let me show you around,' and he took her hand and led her into the kitchen, first on the left.
'Did you do all this yourself?'
'In a way,' he replied.
'Who's the artist?' she asked, pointing around at the leaves and fruits and stems and stalks which peeped through and

wove in and out of the storage units, sink, fridge, cooker and allsorts. The artwork breathed life into the four walls and ceiling, making the box come alive. The wickedly tangy orange of The Orange earthed by the pure green earthy apple. Two stalks made out to be supports for a head high cupboard. All manner of fruitery peered over the fridge. To sum up: the kitchen would delight the most pernickety chef, in mood and equipment.

'Did you do this, Butch?'

'Well I live here, don't I? I'll show you the front room. This way, madam.' With his hand on the lever and just about to open the door, he adds, 'I think we can skip the bedroom, don't you?'

'Yeah, later,' and boy, did she give him a hint. She paused between the two words with the craft of one who has delivered lines effectively for eons. The gap was timed to perfection and would have pleased the most polished performer. But, then again, that's Joanne for you; one big act.

'Maybe never,' he replied.

'Suit yourself.' She barged past him, into the front room. The lever slipped from his hand. She tested the mass of cushions — up against the wall — for softness, by giving them a couple of prods. After nodding her head as a sign of approval, she sank into them. 'Is everything in here yours as well?'

'Yes.'

'You're doing alright.'

'I've just got pieces as I've gone along. You need something to eat off of and something to sleep on. I'm surviving. I mend what breaks. I'm struggling, like everyone else.'

'So you did do the painting. I never knew you had it in you.'

'Well I live here, don't I?'

'How long?'

'Want a drink?'

'What've you got?'

'Vodka.'

'Well, I'll have a vodka then, please.'

'Two weeks,' he answered.

'Well, you couldn't have done the painting. It would take longer than two weeks. Impossible.'

'I've got another two months before the new tenants move in. The woman who used to live here was an artist.' He gave her the vodka. 'I used to do a little business with her. A sistren. She's got locks and everything. But, most times, you'd only find white people round here when you'd come up. They could bubble though. So trade was brisk and the people were alright. She got evicted – I don't think she used to pay the rent – so I moved in.'

'How do you know how long you've got? Have the council been in touch? They're strict on squatting now, aren't they?'

'No. Nothing like that. I know the people who are coming. I was here when they came to view. It's all arranged.'

'Come off it.'

'It's true. A nice young couple. They promised not to change a thing. They loved the artwork. We had a long talk. It was really civil and everything. They bought the vodka and brought it up to celebrate. The man said they'd been waiting three years for a place. Low priority. They weren't really spirit drinkers – they said they preferred beer – and I'm not one for drinking on my own, so they left the bottle; three-quarters full.'

'Students?' she asked.

'No. Down from,' he paused and thought for a while, 'up north somewhere. I can't remember the name of the place. One of those places they call a blackspot. Strange, the guy and his woman were real soft yet the place they come from sounds so hard when you hear things on the television and see things in the papers. They've come down here to work. They've both got jobs. They're alright.'

'They have your seal of approval?'

'They have my seal of approval. He had a bloody nice woman too.'

'You like?'

22

'Only someone who likes punishment gets off on things he can't have.'
'Masochist . . .'
'. . . I am not!'


They made love on the cushions, with the two vodkas on the floor, half drunk. The ice in the glasses fuse with the alcohol, like icebergs disappearing in a scorching ocean. Look anywhere but down, at the vivid rug, like crazy paving and guaranteed to set the head spinning after drinking on an empty stomach. Food was in the house but he couldn't cook; not with a woman there.
Her eyes caught a watch on the television. 'That's a nice watch,' she said. 'Put it on.'
Butch got up, got the watch, put it on and rejoined Joanne on the cushions. She took his wrist in her hands and studied it. 'It looks really nice, Butch. It makes you look right official.'


He dextrously skinned up, slotting the five sheets into position instinctively. 'Put your hand out, palm up.' She did as he instructed and he put the extended skin in her hand. He ran the cigarette down his tongue and placed it on the skin. He ripped the cigarette apart and emptied the tobacco out.
'You have got herbs,' she said.
'No I haven't,' he replied and heaped some fine sensimilia upon the tobacco. He took the spliff from her, rolled it up and fired it. 'Biggre and you in the bedroom,' he prompted, out of the blue and passed the spliff to Joanne.
'This is really turning you on, isn't it?'
'Yeah. Love it. What happened?'
'Picture this,' she started to giggle and gave the spliff back to Butch. 'Weed gives me the giggles.'
'I don't know what you're talking about. Go on,' he replied.
'What have you got between your fingers, Butch?' She still giggled.
'A cigarette.'

23

'Trust no one, eh, Butch,' she gave him a sly wink and tapped her nose.

'Dead right.'

'Dangermouse.'

'Hardly. Taking drugs is illegal.'

'Right. Anyway, me and Biggre are in the baby's bedroom. Damon's in the cot staring up at his dad. Sharon's got all these things hooked up to the cot. There's mobiles and those coloured boxes that play tunes and stuff. You know, you pull the string and they play a nursery rhyme. I've got to describe this to you so that you get the full picture.'

'Go on.'

'Well, this is what happened.'

'What is this a soap opera or something?'

'Alright. Damon's got four of these music boxes down one side of his cot. The mobile hangs over the top; above his head when he's sleeping. Sharon's got him one of those mahogany looking cots. All carved and stuff. It's nice. She's into colours to stimulate Damon. It's not mad. The patterns co-ordinate. The buffer, sheet, quilt, everything. It's sweet. Anyway, all the boxes play different tunes; London bridge, Baa baa black sheep, One two three four five once I caught a fish; all different ones. I think one even plays a selection. They're all very colourful. Well, they're designed to hold a child's attention. There's millions in toys. It's big business. You should get into toys, Butch.'

'Steal from children?'

'I know you wouldn't. Let me tell you.'

'Go on.'

'One of these mobiles is a green elephant with pink dots and while the tune's playing its ears move up and down. Oh yes, and its trunk goes from side to side. Then there's another one like a flower.'

'It either is a flower or it isn't.'

'It's a flower and the petals move in and out. I think it's yellow and red,' she said and placed her index finger on her chin and looked skyward for inspiration, thinking hard. Her cracked nail lay snugly in her dimple. Her permed hair is parted down the centre and hangs shaggily, disguising the roundness of her face. Her cheeks are smattered with freckles. One or two are on her nose and forehead. Her cheeks are alive with them. She could be cute but she seems tired. She could be smart but she seems gullible. It's in her face. A little tired and somewhat uncertain.

Before they do it again, he's going to ask her to brush her teeth.

'Well, there are all these musical things plus the mobile which is about a dozen things in itself. It's got shapes hanging from it. And plays its own tune. Biggre wound up every single one and had them all going at the same time. All at once. Can you imagine it. Little Dame must have thought his cot was being invaded. He just lay there, freaked, looking up to his dad for help. His eyes were saying, get me out of this. In the melee of mechanical music and movement, that kid was looking up to his dad for help. His dad was the tormentor in chief. Biggre's the one who needs help.'

'Maybe. But there's no shame in that. Instability is *the* epidemic nowadays.'

'That's alright for you to say. You're not a defenceless child.'

'Who says so.'

'You haven't got Biggre for a father. It was like something out of a Hitchcock film. Biggre frightened me.'

'I wouldn't have believed that from your performance today.'

'He makes me so mad I don't know what I'm doing. You know what it's like when someone makes you see red.'

'Not really.'

'You've never got angry?'

'Plenty of times but I've never been out of control.'

'Maybe not,' she said, again placing her finger in the dimple and realising that in all the time she's known him — it's true — she's never seen him get mad. Mad, like Hangman could get mad and want to cut and cut and cut. She's surprised at being unable to recall hearing Butch even cuss bad. She killed off her vodka in one swig.

'More?' he asked.

'Thanks,' she replied and he took her glass, got up and went to refill it.

'I don't know how it happened. All I can remember is yelling, Biggre, don't you care about your son? The next thing we were in bed. He said he cared though, I remember that too.' She paused momentarily, struck by what her mouth told her ears. 'Weird,' she said introspectively and paused again. 'But that doesn't make me his woman. It doesn't give him the right to tell me how to live my life. It was only once. Don't you think he's even the least bit crazy, Butch?'

And he dropped the glass.

'I suppose I'll have to clean that up,' she concluded.

# The Seaman

Patrick travelled all over the world as a seaman.
He does odd jobs around the pub; collecting glasses, cleaning
up, opening up and sometimes serving; whatever jobs Jenny
and Pete, who run the pub for a brewery, can't be bothered
with.
When he was younger he was a handsome man. He opened
doors for ladies. He never swore in mixed company. 'The
world would be impossible were it not for the gentler sex,' he
mused on more than one occasion. 'Fact,' he concluded. He,
as a connoisseur, surely knows better than anyone the ways
of a woman. And as with all connoisseurs, he believed he
could tell the charlatan from the true artiste easily. Experience.
That's the key.

So he sailed the seas in search of his nirvana,
the geisha.
He voyaged to the Orient,
his dreams end,
a dozen times or more
for her.
And she would come singing and dancing into his eyes.
She, clad in silk embroidered with shimmering threads in
sparkling colours,
making faces and trees,
great emperors and goddesses.
She, who kneads his body with her hands,

before softening and soothing it with oils of the sweetest
perfume.
Ah, and she who is
as only
she
can be.


The last place he'd been to was the Cape. He was on a ship
carrying fruit. Nobody wanted him after that trip, so he had
to pack up the navy lark. The cops caught him with a black
woman. Shit, you'd have thought they loved the lady from
the way they carried on. It was like a man catching his wife
with her lover in flagrante delicto.

It was as if the act was being carried out to purposely humiliate
them. They reacted on that personal level and gave Patrick
one hell of a beating, which palls to insignificance in com-
parison to the degradation and physical abuse they saw fit to
afflict upon his partner. He was made to watch and could
only bawl like a helpless child.

After they'd finished, they dragged her by her hair up on
deck then flung her overboard. He was ordered to stay on
board if he wanted to avoid any more trouble. 'There is no
place here for white men who go with kaffa women. It is not
safe for you here. We cannot guarantee your safety, so it's
better you leave,' their leader said, in the presence of the
ship's captain. The captain promised to get rid of Patrick as
soon as he could. 'Good,' their leader said. 'Good.' The captain
gave a crate of Jamaica rum to each of the cops and pledged
himself to the preservation of peace in their beautiful country,
for the remainder of their stay and during future visits. The
leader winked at his men, put his hand on the captain's
shoulder and called him a sensible man of great insight.

Becoming a landlubber after years at sea shook him up badly.
Patrick was part fish. He needed the water to keep himself
together. The exotic East became a thing of the past. The
mysteries and wonder of Africa, a mere memory. The forgotten

28

splendour of Sydney harbour. The worlds of this world were closed to him.

He couldn't find his comb. Someone had ripped it off for a laugh as he shambled around the night before collecting glasses. So he ran his fingers through his hair to try and make it look tidy. He had a lot of hair for his age. The front was quite long and kept falling in front of his eyes. It was thick too. His complexion was dark and rugged, not with the richness of the children of the sun but rich and dark in the accepted European sense. His clothes, although of impeccable quality, had lost their lives some time ago. The materials appeared weary. Oh yes his plimsolls, the yachting type tied with odd coloured laces. Neither of the colours were suitable for the blue canvas, white soled, not out of place in Hampshire plimmies. His jacket is interesting. It aids the impression that he's wearing one of those shirts with the frilly cuffs; he isn't really of course, it's just an impression. The inner lining of his jacket sleeve had run the gamut of dust to dirt then grime and eventually torn. The lining encircles his wrist in a brocade, like frilly cuffs would. For all this, you could not say he was dirty. His face is clean. As I've said, his hair is healthy. Nice hands. And he generally wears a subtle cologne.

*Errol Flynn in his dandy's shirt, unbuttoned to the navel, a cutlass locked in his pearly white teeth. The Adventurer, sailing the seven seas and on into the sunset forevermore. For the stars it never ends.*

Poor old Patrick should have been a star. He'd docked at New York (up north) and Miami (down south). He could have hitched up or across to Hollywood, made it big and lived the buccaneer's life for all it's worth.

On his way to work, he passed Biggre on the street with the garage. They knew one another well enough. When Biggre was with Sharon he drank at the pub. Since they split up he doesn't go so often. He doesn't drink any more either.

Biggre and Patrick once had a lengthy discussion about mine and yours, possessions, at about eight o'clock one Saturday night. There were only a few people about. Their round table attracted a small audience. They swapped ideas and the theory they drew up developed to the ultimate conclusion that the concept of mine and yours and possessions in general should be eradicated, so that all the good things on the earth could benefit the whole of mankind and not just a few people. The ganja salesman made a remark about what he'd do to anyone trying to get his herbs without paying for it. And our boys' ideals (like the stars, we chart our course by them, but can never reach them) went whizzing by, never to be seen again for thousands of years.

One said, 'So, say somebody just walks into your house and takes your food and eats it, or just takes your car and drives away with it, or plays your stereo without permission, even sleeps with your woman, would you be cool? I would kill a man for that! What's mine is mine. Big fish eats little fish.'

And another countered, defending Biggre and Pat, 'Yes, you might feel that way at the time, or because you've been conditioned to, but it's out of materialism and possessiveness that you would commit murder. See the war films. See the archives. Big men in trenches crying like babies. You think killing is as simple as that. It's not. We're all going to leave with nothing. Ashes to ashes, dust to dust.'

'I've heard of places in Africa where everything is shared. Everything is shared within the tribe,' Patrick added.

A white bloke at the bar yelled, 'Crawler,' half jokingly. Pause, tension, but nothing happens.

Pete came over and with a tone of finality said, 'Look, I

don't care what anybody says, people like to keep what they've got and have always been willing to fight for survival. And that means protecting what's theirs. Patrick, you've got work to do.'

The ganja salesman grabbed Patrick's hand and with a deft snatch had his ring from his finger. 'It's mine now because I say it is, it's not yours and according to you it never was.'

'Give the man his ring back,' wailed the eloquent but weak defender.

The ganja guy strutted out of the pub putting a shine on his new ring, holding it delicately between his thumb and forefinger as he polishes it with his sleeve.

'You're a fool to yourself, Patrick. That guy's bad news. You can kiss your ring goodbye.' Pete went back to the bar to serve.

On this particular day as their paths crossed, Biggre simply said, 'White man' to him, in a particularly sombre and deep voice. It never shook him up but it was something Patrick nonetheless noted. He also passed Derrick, who said nothing to him. It seemed as though Derrick hadn't seen him or better still looked right through him. Patrick had always assumed that for D, *The Hope* scene was a passing phase. To him, D always appeared well earthed. On this day, he wasn't his usual self. To be honest, Patrick doesn't normally even think about shouting at black guys on the street but on this occasion for a split second, he did.

Around here, the very idea of a white man shouting at blacks, for any reason, smacks of them thinking they are over us. It's a matter difficult to deal with. Patrick has deduced from his wealth of experience that matters of pride are to be dealt with delicately. And you know what they say, 'I didn't know what being down was like, until I'd been there myself.'

Patrick knew rejection well.

Jenny and Pete have had to go out so Patrick is to open up for early evening trade. He dug the big bunch of keys Pete had given to him out of his pocket. His personal keys came up too, hooked up to the big bunch and fell on the ground. He'd pick them up after sorting out getting inside.

There were all sorts of keys on the big bunch; yales, mortice, big padlock, little padlock, even a key with notches going in two directions. In all there must have been two dozen keys. He stared at them, then at the door, back to the keys again and ran his fingers through his hair, perplexed.

The door had two locks at about door handle height, one at the bottom and one at the top. Patrick knew that once the door was opened the alarm would go off and one of the keys in his hand stopped it. If the alarm went on for too long, Rusty, the doberman out in the yard, would break loose from his restraining chain and set about the intruder, as he's been trained to. See 'em off. Sik im. Sik im.

Patrick started to go over Pete's run down on which keys to use for each of the locks. He again looked at the keys, then the locks but this time he began to sweat. 'He'll kill me,' he murmured.

In the end what he actually did was go through all the keys at random until the door opened. Fortunately the key to stop the alarm was an obvious choice. It was the one with the twin notches. Instinctively he walked to the yard door, opened the curtain, looked straight into the dog's red eyes and said, 'Starve!' As expected Rusty had elevated himself to about Patrick's height by propping himself up on the door by his front legs. Although he's trained not to break the chain until the alarm sounds, he's ready at the first turn of a key in the front door. Rust's a fascist, you know. You can tell by the way he sticks out his chest and wallows in the depth of his own meanness. He's a right dog is Rusty. He'll be cool with Patrick though because he can see that his entry is legal. And the face is familiar. And no bells, which helps. It's the bells that really set him off.

Patrick went to close the door. The BMW drew up opposite. T Boy rolled down the window, smiled at Patrick and gave him the thumbs up sign. It drizzled lightly for a noticeable second. Patrick looked up then closed the door. T Boy poked his head out and looked up too. Patrick heard the BMW draw away and sighed a huge sigh of relief.
Shit, those boys are bad.

# Everylittlebithurts

## 10

'Is that you, Bill?'

'No. It's me,' Derrick answered.

His mother appeared and lodged herself in the half opened front room doorway. Derrick's home is further away from *The Hope* than Butch's place. His is a bus ride away, although he walked it today; alone, brooding. At a brisk pace it can be walked in twenty minutes to half an hour. His family have owned the house they live in since before he was born. They bought it a short while after Eric, the eldest, came into the world. There are people on his street he's known all his life and the other way round.

'Do you want me to leave?' he asked.

'Didn't I tell you not to use the front door. Your room is in the basement. Use the door down there.'

'I didn't open the door. I met it open.'

'It wasn't open to you.'

'Do you want me to leave?'

'You and your thieving friends. If you can call some of the animals that turn up here, friends,' she said scornfully and kissed her teeth.

'Only one person comes round here that could fit that description. Taking it that you don't mean females, it could only be Butch, again, couldn't it?'

'What sort of decent woman would want you? Seeing you hanging around with that. I would die of shock if I ever saw a woman come here for you. She would need her brains tested. Who else could it be but that ragamuffin.'

Bill came up the stairs, behind D. 'Alright, son,' he said.

'Yeah. I'm alright, dad.'

'Good, good,' and he squeezed past his son and into the passage.

The front room was off the passage, on the right hand side. Bill gave his wife a peck on the cheek. 'Don't forget we've got to be at the cricket club by seven.' He carried on through the passage, up the stairs to two bedrooms and a bathroom on the top floor of their two storey and basement home. There's a shower and toilet in the basement too.

'Your suit's still in the cleaners. I forgot to get it on my way home,' she shouted after him.

'I'd better go and get it then,' and he turned, retraced his steps to the front door, saying, 'Excuse me, son,' as he breezed back out.

'Do you want me to leave?' Derrick asked.

'You're a bloody disgrace. Don't you think I know what you and your friend get up to,' she replied.

'What do we get up to?'

'You're a weed seller,' she stated, pointing an accusing finger at him and fighting frantically with the smile that lay behind her frowning expression. The power of the smile rippled through her cheeks and tweeked at the corners of her lips. If only he'd run up, throw his arms around her and give her a peck like he used to just a few years ago, which seems like just the other day. If only he'd give her the chance to meet him half way like he used to. 'D used to treat me as if I were his daughter. He acted as if he were my protector and would give anything to see me happy,' she thought. 'Look at him standing there as belligerent as a bull. He's so dogmatic now.'

'I've never sold weed and anybody who says I have is a liar.'

'So I'm a liar then?'

'If you think I sell weed you're wrong.'

'Look. Get out, boy,' she ordered beggingly. Go soon before my facade slips completely and acting as your child run into your arms, she meant. The spasm in her cheeks tugged violently at her lips, causing them to ripple and surely reveal the subjacent smile.

But sure as eggs is eggs he wouldn't let up. 'Do you want me to leave?'

'In future just remember to use the basement door,' she said and went back in the front room, closing the door behind her.

Derrick's mother sat in the couch. She's given up on waiting for the tuneful rat a tat tat, followed by the cheeky face — pulled in some funny form — peering round to make her laugh and diffuse any bad vibes. That was the traditional style of their rows. That pattern is history. She unwrapped her head scarf and began to undo the rollers in her hair. Her and Derrick haven't had a calm conversation for at least six months. To Derrick it seems as though they haven't seen one another six times in as many months but he can't see her standing back slightly from the front room window or behind the net curtain in the bedroom at night, watching his comings and goings and making sure she sees him once a day at the very least. No matter the sly and wily way she has to go about it. She thought the ice would have broken long ago. But no! Derrick is quite content to perceive her and his father as — at best — parental landlords. Bill says it's nothing, yet she firmly believes that their son is cutting them out of his life and filling their role with people who are no good. It's their influence which fuels her fears. That boy Butch in particular. That boy Butch. 'He looks like a tramp. He's got no family and he's wild. The wildness comes from lack of parental guidance and supervision.'

By the time she'd freed the last roller, which incidentally (sods law being what it is) took almost as long to undo as all the others put together, the smile had surfaced. After all, she'd been waiting for an opportunity to hear her son's voice and give him the once over from close range since their last encounter about a month ago and had succeeded at last. The smile grew and grew, evolved cocoon to caterpillar to butterfly

like, until it became full and hearty. Her laughter travelled
through the window and out the door into the street. From
outside-looking-in, all that could be made out was the sil-
houette of a woman pulling at her hair and chortling wildly
for no apparent reason. She's got a laugh like Bette Davis.
There's more than one angle to it. Which is true enough, for
although she's satisfied at the moment, she's only won a
battle and not the war. She knows nothing's really changed.
The war continues. It's the quaint laughter of the vanquished.
She hasn't got back into his life only intruded for a while,
that's all. Plus he was more distant than normal.

'Olive, what are you doing? People passing by are looking up
at our window,' Bill said in his own light way and gently
shook her out of it.
'Oh, Bill,' she sprang up and threw her arms around him.
He dropped the suit, held her close and caressed her.

## 11

Nobody knows much about Naomi. She's just a name to all
of them. The distinct lack of information they have on her is
a bridge between Butch and Derrick's mother and father. His
mother tries to get more info out of him in subtle, not so
subtle and sometimes bluntly intrusive ways but D deflects
her in whichever way is appropriate to the approach. And in
all truth what he could tell them, if he opened up, wouldn't
amount to much anyway. The picture he'd paint of her would

have no depth and simply skirt on the periphery. He'd portray a fleeting acquaintance. A shallow illustration, an outline, a sketch of someone he'd come in contact with a couple of times. He would evoke infatuation, not love.

Hangman's a shit and he's going to get his!

In a way Naomi is only an acquaintance of Derrick's. How many times have they dated? Once a week or less since they got to know one another, meeting on their way home from school; each walking their own way; as we know is D's manner (to keep to himself) and now we can assume is Naomi's too. Derrick took to her immediately he saw her; all neat and tidy and quiet. Especially her quietness, because that's the sign of a good girl who doesn't mess around.

He had her within a week of their first meeting and hasn't got anywhere near a replay since. It's no surprise really when consideration is given to the trials he undergoes simply to see her. When they can, they meet in the street and walk around. This is usually either on her way home from work or during a lunchbreak. Lunchbreaks are difficult because it means he has to get up to the city where she works in an office full of snooty stockbrokery types and soulboys and girls imperson-ating them. He swears one of those curly perm boys sniggers and makes comments. He was once going to go down there and shut him up for good, but Naomi dissuaded him by explaining that if he did she'd be sacked. People laugh at the curly heads behind their backs, she told him. They're not going anywhere. Some stockies make jokes about black this and black that and the curlies are the first to laugh, she told him. And then they tell the straight head boys that they can take a joke, and they're alright, unlike some of their brothers, she told him. Then the curly straight super slick dick starts to explain about the way he was brought up and associations and associations and he didn't know any black guy who couldn't take a joke, but it's because of the way he was brought up and associations and associations. So Derrick let the boy off, on compassionate grounds. Additionally, he

39

didn't have the bus fare. What she didn't tell him was that the Straight Head in Chief was her boyfriend. She never told him that.

Derrick held Naomi in such high esteem that Butch never mentioned her name without the straightest of faces. He neither ribbed Derrick about her or asked to meet the precious piece of pussy. His attitude bordered on the reverential, which is out of character for Our Butch. He was suspicious.

Naomi's parents treated D like scum, or so he thought. They might have been doing him a favour. Even giving him hints and putting him on the right track. They probably knew all about the straight head. They've probably had him round to dinner. When he rang, according to whichever parent answered the phone, she wouldn't be in nor would they know when she could be expected. Get the acting from these two extreme mama and papaites. Protective aint the word. He was sure her parents had told her supervisor to keep him away from her. It was a hunch Naomi put down as her supervisor's natural reaction to his blunt manner and no way would her parents go that far. I mean, didn't her daddy find her the job, sit in on her interview, take her to work every day for the first six months and collect her frequently at the beginning. An exaggeration, maybe the first two or three months, but it felt like a year to D because he couldn't wait for big daddy to let go. But as I say, the man might have been doing him a favour.

Derrick's first thought after the altercation with his mother was to ring his woman and get things off his chest. She'd still be at work. His mother's in so he can't get to the phone and make a sneak call. Even if she wasn't he'd have to rely on her forgetting to unplug it and lock it away. (A practice she'd adopted during Butch's brief board and ceased for a time after he'd left, but resumed now that her and D are on bad terms.) Getting to the phone wasn't a certainty whether she was there or not. It's not the same as with Butch though. She hid the phone from him because she couldn't stand him. For her son it was a carrot. When D is forced to ask for the phone, she'll have seen and spoken to him. Best of all he'll be asking for something.

On his way to the phone boxes, D saw his dad hanging around in the dry cleaners on the opposite side of the road. He was looking out the glass front into the street with his back to the counter.

Derrick waved and asked, 'Not ready yet?' referring to the suit; forming his mouth around the words to clearly show what he was saying. He wasn't shouting.

His father nodded.

Derrick pointed down the road at the boxes to show Bill where he was going.

Bill nodded and turned around to see if the woman had found his suit. The woman said it was done but she couldn't find it and Bill hadn't heard a word D had said and he'd forgotten to get the cleaning ticket from Olive which didn't aid expediency. The woman knew Bill and Olive and the kids as they'd been going to this particular cleaners since it opened. They could remember when it was a bakery. The suit had been done at the cleaners plenty of times. The woman kept saying things like, 'It's got to be here somewhere. I'll find it in a minute. Now, it's a blue suit, isn't it?'

And Bill would nod and say, 'Yes.'

And she'd say, 'It's got to be here somewhere. You said, blue. I'll find it in a minute. It got to be here. Blue,' she muses on the colour.

D reached the boxes; three of them all in a row outside the BT building, adjacent to the post office and across the road from the fish and chip shop. The location of the boxes has no doubt been determined by much market research and analysis into suitable positions for the siting of public call boxes to serve the area. Surveys to find a favourable point within a designated catchment area. Somewhere not too out of the way and designed in an unintimidating way so that people aren't afraid to use them casually. A prime spot to provide maximum returns on investment. They've got it right 'cos the boxes are well used. The glazing is inscribed ad hoc with messages and mini biogs, such as: WEST HAM FA CUP WINNERS 81, with an etched icon of the club's motif (two hammers crossed); RING MANDY, on such and such a number, for the ultimate lessons in love; and what about this one, EXPERIENCED DISCIPLINARIAN AVAILABLE, for administering corporal punishment, slipper, cane; RING HARRY, again on such and such a number, with no reason given, just ring, please, I only need someone to talk to. Then you've got the usual innocent ones like two names with the associated etched heart and arrow, and DON WOZ ERE 81, and loads of other indecipherable mis-spelt notes and tele-phone numbers without names and names without numbers. All this is innocuous enough if you're good at ignoring things and unattracted by useless bits of information. (Half the numbers are bogus, the other half, cries for attention in an unattentive world.) But how do you nullify your sense of smell? How do you close your nose? The urine trickles out underneath the doors to the pavement and on into the gutter. The used johnny bags fester in dirty corners. Cigarette butts and torn directory pages carpet the floor. Today's heat has concentrated the highly-rancid mixture in the glass bowl.

Two people wait for one box while the other two are empty. 'Probably messed up,' he thought. But desperate for the solace at the other end of the line he still tried them. In the first box, the lead connecting the handset to the coin box and dial had been crudely severed. It must have been done with one brutal tug because the exposed wires are jagged and of odd lengths. The box reeked of piss. He opened the second door and the smell sent him reeling back. The coin box was a complete mess. Someone had walked off with the receiver. Derrick joined the queue, at the back. Immediately the first user came out and the queue was reduced by one.

He's standing in line behind a man wearing a broad brimmed

hat. The man watched him make a fool of himself trying the other boxes. He could have said they were out of order. The man was skylarking. A slight drizzle comes down. The man looks from side to side; looking at everybody else getting wet; all smug and flash and so much like Soulboy or Hangers. 'Make the mistake of looking at me,' Derrick pleaded mentally. The flash man casually glanced at him all superior like, in response to D's plea. Derrick grabbed the man's head from the back, between his two hands. Holding it like an oval object, like a big egg, and slammed it against the kiosk several times. Then he backed away and kicked the man off the kiosk to sprawl on the sidewalk. 'Bastard!' D kicked him in the ribs. 'Flash bastards!' and he kicked the man again as he scrambled to his feet and retreated from D, hobbling. 'Who's going to kill who?' Derrick barked.

When he turned the phone box was empty.

He kicked the man's hat into the gutter.

He shoved his coin through the slot, sending it whizzing noisily through the system. He dialled the number and connected without any ringing. 'Hello. Is Naomi there?' he asks.

'She's in a meeting,' came the crisp reply. It was her Super.

'How long do you think she'll be?'

'It's a very important meeting and they do pay her to work for them until six o'clock.'

'So it looks as if she's busy then.'

'I think we can safely assume that.'

'Could you give her a message for me, please? I'm in a tricky situation and I need to speak to her urgently.'

'What? Are you in some sort of trouble?'

He snapped, 'Why don't you mind your own business. I'm not in any trouble.'

'I thought you said you were. Anyway, I haven't got all day. What's the bloody message? Why don't you leave her alone?'

'Because she loves me.'

It sounded as if the supervisor was broadcasting this to the

43

whole office block through a megaphone. The people across the street from the kiosk, in the fish and chip shop must have heard this one and borne testament to his shame. 'Loves you? You fool. She's got a bloke here. You're a pest. Why don't you just bloody leave her alone. She doesn't want people like you ruining her life.'

'Tell her, I'm dead!' and he replaced the receiver as if it were priceless; nice and gently. And slowly left the box and started down the road, heading home.

<br>

## 12

It's eight. Another hour to go.

Derrick lay on his bed and stared up at the ceiling. His bag was packed and ready. His mother and father have gone out to the club. They didn't say bye or anything. He heard the front door close, the click clacking of his mother's heels down the concrete steps, the car doors open and close, the car start up and drive away, that's how he knew. But he never thought anything of it. Although his dad usually says something, even if it's only shouting 'There's no one upstairs' last thing before he closes the door and turns off. Derrick was only conscious of his moving away from them, their movements didn't register. He hadn't seen Bill hug Olive and comfort her saying, 'He's big enough to look after himself. We've raised him the best way we know how, now leave it. It's our chance to have a life. Let him go.'

And heard her say, 'I'm worried about him.'

'So am I. But I worry from afar. We must worry in silence. Give him space he'll be alright.'

'Okay,' she said.

'Are you alright now?' he asked.

'Yes. I'm fine. We'd better hurry else we'll be late.' She made to move away and get off to tidy herself.

He held her back. 'We're late already. Why rush? Time's on our side. We haven't got any babies. Our time is our own.'

Derrick isn't as zealous in his tidiness as Butch but he's okay. He isn't into emptying the ashtray after every cigarette or folding and packing away everything in sight but there is a definite sense of organisation about his room. The room itself is a fair old size. A double bedroom, I think. Some would say that D is fortunate; born the other side of the tracks. For him though, it isn't enough. Of what? I don't know. Maybe he doesn't consider himself fortunate at all. The clock on his chest of drawers which kept his socks, shirts and odds and sods ticked steadily towards nine. The relentless, monotonous ticking and tocking, back and forth beat, beat out like a roll of thunder in the absolute silence of D's home.

He saw a thousand clockwork soldiers marching across the whitewash sky. Arms and legs moving stiffly in time. Tick tock, tick tock, tick tock tick. DEATH OR GLORY, BOYS. Into the valley.

*The dancing glint of steel in the sunlight on an open field as the first sabre's drawn and the dashing young lieutenant cries, 'Forward to victory!' and sails off on his steed, heading straight to the heart of the opposing army and his opposite number.*

This is how it has to be. It's all about pride. It's him or me. Hangman and Derrick, it's got to happen because D doesn't like backing down again and again. And the clock's the only sound that can be heard. Derrick's stripped bare to the waist with Naomi on his mind.

He thought of their one and only time. That was IT for him. He's bathed in that occasion once a day religiously since it happened. Even with someone else, it's her looking up at him from the pillow and her eyes into which he drowns, helpless like a soft fluffy pussycat.

But then again it could be avoided honourably. 'She wouldn't want to know,' he said, breaking the clock's monopoly. If it came to chopping up, she wouldn't want to know him. The blag's the answer. LA can't be all bad. He could take Naomi. He'd be with friends. Hit and run. The job comes first, personal vendettas second. 'Scavengers,' he said. 'I'll show them. I'll be made after tonight. Screw them!' If you knew D well you could tell he was being half-hearted. Most of all he still wanted Hangman's balls.

He would be cool for Naomi. He decided to go and get her after they'd split the money and leave one time. He smiled at the thought of more daring intentions of a different strain. The two of them clambering down a ladder propped under her bedroom window. She, dressed in an overcoat over her nightdress and barefoot. He, struggling to keep balanced and hurriedly descending the ladder with two packed and bulging suitcases; one in his hand, the other under his arm, one hand free to hold the ladder.

'If I could only have the best of both worlds,' he thought.

'Next time I'm going to kill you, huh,' he repeated Hangman's threat scornfully. 'I'll get that bastard.' He pulled something long and thin and wrapped in newspaper from under his mattress and put it in his bag. 'No one does that to me.'

D flashed on his shirt, shoes and jacket as if he'd had a handful of amphetamines. It's eight thirty as D picks up his bag and sets off for Butch's place.

# 13

D tunefully tapped on Butch's door.

'Enter,' Butch shouted, all dramatic and ham actor style.

Derrick knew the routine for getting in and went through it automatically. He dropped his bag by the front door (in the lobby) and walked straight to the front room. Butch was dressed and sitting on the cushions doing up his laces. The room smelt of sex. The cushions were numb and lifeless, not their usual selves. The two glasses Butch and Joanne had drunk from were still on the floor beside Butch's feet. One glass was unfinished. The bottle on the shelf was empty. All tell tale signs to D. 'So you did then?'

'Now that would be telling, wouldn't it?' Butch replied as he passed Derrick, taking the glasses into the kitchen.

Derrick hung round the front room door and didn't really go into the room; not right in. He was in but not in, if you get what I mean. 'We've only got a couple of minutes,' he said.

'I'll tidy this place in a couple of seconds. Swiftness D, swiftness.'

Derrick didn't budge. He didn't react. He didn't laugh at his brother's little joke or screw up his face as if to say, 'Call that a joke?', or say, 'Very funny,' with sarcasm on overload. It was as if the words went through him.

'Hey! It's only across the park. I can't leave the place like this. We'll be there before time. What's up? Are you alright?'

'Yes, I'm cool. Why are you cleaning? You've had a woman up here.'

'I don't need someone to wipe my bum for me.'

'In fact I'd say Joanne's been here.' He waited for a denial or confirmation but it never came.

'Watch it,' Butch advised softly.

'Watch what?'

'Watch yourself,' he returned to the front room and started puffing up the cushions.

'What do you mean?'

47

'You're degenerating, D.'

'You're degenerating, D,' Derrick scoffed.

'See what I mean.'

'Hey, just tell me straight. Do you want me in on this or don't you?'

'What do you mean? Let's go.'

'You've been on my back all day, Butch. Why?'

'What do you mean, on your back?'

'Do you want me in on this or don't you?' Derrick again asked, sounding frustrated in his relentless search for a yes or a no.

'Cool down, D. Cool down.'

'I know you think I'm the big dumb one and you're the one with all the brains.'

'What are you talking about. That's crap. You're talking to me Derrick, Butch,' and he prodded himself.

'Don't take me for a ride.'

'Who me?' Butch went back to the kitchen and returned with the unfinished vodka. 'Here. Drink. I was going to leave it 'til I came back. Here. Drink.' D wouldn't take the glass from him. 'It's me, Butcher. Your brother, Butch. Come on, drink, it'll steady you down.'

'I don't need steadying,' he said and took the drink and flung it back. It scorched his throat and he coughed in uncontrollable spurts.

'Okay now?'

Derrick nodded and smiled.

'Anyway, do I ask what you and Naomi get up to in bed.'

'Let's go,' D said in a splutter. He put the empty glass in the kitchen and picked up his bag. Butch looked about the room. He shook his head, dissatisfied at the state he'd have to leave it in. As far as Naomi's concerned, he left well alone as he'd always done on that topic.

As they started down the steps Butch asked, 'What's in the bag?'

# Heroes

## 14

The fur warehouse came into view when they turned right at the bottom of the short road off the alley, which runs up the side of the town hall. The alley is well lit but the side streets off it are quite dark. There are only a few street lamps. Their light is a subdued soft yellow. The warehouse has a sheer outline. It's not much more than a square shape in brick. The windows and doors are inset flush. There are no ledges to encourage the aspiring cat burglar.

'Is this place wired up?' asked Derrick.

Butch pointed up at the green box perched high on the wall.

'So what are we doing here? Can you do alarms?'

'My sparks will be here soon,' Butch replied.

'Who's your sparks?'

'Wait and see. Wait and see.'

'You're acting strange today, Butch,' Derrick said with a grin.

Butch echoed his friend's sentiments and grin. He returned a larger grin than the one he was given. The boys looked at each other and chuckled together. Hearing unsaid words.

'Strange day.' Butch flung his arm over D's shoulder.

'Very.'

*The great good guy of a thousand flicks sits cross-legged on the earth before a crackling brushwood fire. His red man friend sits facing him; bronzed, muscular and lithe looking. The red man's hair is braided. There's a colourful feather popping up from the back of his skull, kept in place by the obligatory headband. The flickering fire's light floods the scene in a stuttering crimson and cuts an opening in the darkness, so that only they are made visible by its glowing. In this land where the pioneer treads fearfully, the good guy of a million scenes and dreams comes and goes as he pleases. His chic buckskin suit and stetson; packing two gleaming guns; flashing his flowing long blond hair and sparkling teeth to all, a friend. They look into each other's eyes and pass the knife between them, slashing wrists then pressing them together, letting their blood mingle. Hi Ho Silver.*

'So when is the sparks going to get here?'
'Should be here any minute,' Butch replied.
'I don't want to hang around for too long.'
'He'll be here soon.'
'Do I know him?'
'He'll be here in a minute,' Butch reasserted.
'I'm going for a walk.'
'Where to? He'll be here in the next couple of minutes.' He looked at his watch.
'I've never seen you wearing a watch before. Gone all professional. Synchronise watches etcetera.'
'He'll be here soon.'
'Trying to convince yourself? If he isn't here real soon, I'm taking a hike. We can't just stand around waiting to burgle. Shit, Butch. We'll be standing around waiting to get in when people start turning up for work in the morning.'
'That's not such a bad idea,' adjudged Butch. 'We'll go home, have a good night's kip, come back when the factory opens seven o'clock tomorrow morning, walk in with the workers, go into the office, take the goodies and leave. I like things kept simple.' Butch stopped, again looked at his watch and said, 'Let's give him another couple of minutes.'
'He'd better show soon.' Derrick spat on the ground.
'What's with all the spitting, D? Are we common crooks.' He emphasised the common.
'It's Hangman. I just can't get over the way ...'

50

'If you don't want to get yourself killed, you'd better start getting over quick.'

'He's nothing, Butch. Nothing.'

'He has a sword, Derrick. A sword. Sometimes you've got to roll with the punches.'

'Forget it. I can look after myself.'

'I DO look after myself and as I'm the one with actual savvy I strongly recommend a bad dose of amnesia as the way out of your hassles with Hangers.'

'I don't want a way out. Forget it.'

'Okay. It's your life.'

'That's right.' He paused. 'Hangman.' He spat. 'I'll hang him!'

'Did you hear that?'

'Hear what?'

'Footsteps.'

'No. It's in your mind. Like this whole non event. In your mind.'

'Shhh,' and they stopped talking. Butch listened intently for the direction the steps — he could hear clearly — were taking. D stood around all disaffected like, spitting and pretending to be disinterested. Butch looked D up and down as the lumps like missiles flew out of his mouth to explode and splatter on the ground. D ejected the gob-like darts; hard and fast. Spit spat split splat splash.

'What if it's the Bill? We can get done for loitering with intent.'

'They'll have to prove it. I only live on the other side of the park. This is my neighbourhood.'

'Sure,' Derrick cynically replied. 'I'm taking a walk.'

'The steps are coming this way. It's him.'

'It could be anybody. Butch, we shouldn't be caught just standing around.' D's face perspired slightly.

'You're sweating, D. Have you got the bottle?'

'No. Better than that.' He produced a mallet and moved quickly to the end of the block — at the turning — and stood with his back pressed against the wall. The mallet was raised high, ready to crash down on the cranium of any unwelcome observer to turn the corner of the short road off the alley.

'What's all this?' Butch said aghast but not loud enough for his friend to hear. He moved up to his friend and instinctively also pressed himself up against the wall. Like you see the soldiers doing in Ireland on the TV. It was a subconscious and imitative action because he knew he had nothing to fear. He was ninety-five per cent certain of who's footsteps he heard. 'Calm down,' he whispered in D's ear. 'Are you going to use that thing?' he asked nodding in the direction of the mallet.

'If I need to.'

'Only one person walks like that, Derrick.'

D became more accustomed to the sound. 'What! Not him. Why didn't you say anything this afternoon. If I'd known this joker would be involved I wouldn't even have thought about it.'

'I know,' said Butch.

'No matter. He'll do.' D kept the mallet raised menacingly.

'He's on our side.'

'I hope you know what you're doing.' He relaxed and lowered the mallet, smiled at Butch and went back down the road.

'I do,' Butch replied. 'I've got it all worked out.'

The shape appeared. Footsteps made flesh. It was the irrepressible one. The Flame. Biggre was back. He was dressed from head to toe in black. Black polo neck, black cords and black trainers. No. The trainers had white flashes down the sides. (For a bit of style from the master of multiple modes, maybe.)

'You're late. Where's the motor, Biggre?'

'I fell asleep. The car's parked up the road, not far. And no names, please. From now on, no names. It's essential.' He brushed past Butch. He walked up to Derrick, who was sitting on the ground outside the warehouse with his bag beside him. 'Derrick,' he said, meaning hello and listen.

'B,' D replied.

'No names from now on, agreed?'

'Agreed.'

Biggre looked up at the alarm. 'How much is this worth?'

Butch replied, 'It must be five a piece at the least.'

'Five what? Pence?'

'Five grand.'

'If that's what you mean, why don't you just say it plain.'

Biggre looked at the building then at Derrick. 'Piece of cake.'

'Talking to me?' Derrick asked. 'Talking about me?' He went into his bag and was getting up.

'Hot, hot, hot. I was talking about the alarm, Killer.'

'Don't mess, Madman.' D sat back down. 'Hey, Butch, let's get on with it.'

'No names. No names,' Biggre said annoyedly. 'If your buddy can't get the point we'd better drop it.' He huffed and puffed.

'Alright,' Butch replied and went and squatted beside his friend. He spoke softly in D's ear. 'Keep it cool, man. I want to get it over and done with too. Are you alright?'

'I'm alright.'

And Butch caught on. 'Put it out of your mind. Hangers is rubbish. They're all rubbish. Remember that. Rubbish.'

'I know.'

Butch kissed his teeth. 'Do you want to die?'

'Does anybody?'

'I don't know. Do you?'

'No. Hangman's the one that's going to die. I'll see to that. I'll see to that.'

'Give it up.'

'Let's get on with it, Butch.'

'No names.'

'Okay, okay. Now let's get on with it. Get what we came for and piss off.' With that D sprang to his feet and spat.

Butch looked over to Biggre and asked him if he was ready. But Biggre had got off on his petulant act and didn't reply. He continued to huff and puff. His arms were folded across his chest and he looked at the pavement as he kicked it alternately with either foot, scuffing his immaculate trainers. It was a strange sight. It seemed as if he were doing a little jig. It appeared as though he were dancing.

Derrick went up close to his mate and muttered, 'I asked you if you were sure. You said yes,' then sat back down.

Biggre cast his eye over Derrick and Derrick eyeballed him back.

One of Biggre's legs was slightly shorter than the other. Thus each kick made his body move like a piston. He was going up on the longer leg then down on the shorter one.

Biggre's upper lip touched his nose in a pronounced facial expression of complete annoyance.

Biggre walked away.

'Where are you going?' Butch asked.

Biggre didn't answer. He stopped over the road from the building.

Derrick looked up at Butch and said, 'He's mad.'

'He's not the only one,' Butch replied. 'What are you doing?' he called to Biggre. Biggre continued to ignore him and bent over to pick up pebbles. He selected some and kept them. Butch, looking at Biggre, shook his head in exasperation, then glanced at his watch anxiously.

'Forget about synchronising watches, Butch. You want to synchronise his brain,' said Derrick.

'No names.'

'Sorry, I forgot. Got the cyanide capsules?'

They both laughed.

'When's he going to get started?' D asked.

'Search me.'

'He's playing with stones. We want to break into this place and he's playing with stones. Are you sure about him? Did you check?'

'I know he's on the level,' Butch said with certainty in his voice, but uncertainty in the way he scratched his head and looked bemused over at Biggre, now leaning against the opposing warehouse and tossing the pebbles from hand to hand. Butch started over to Biggre to find out if it was going to happen or not.

'Get some stones,' said Biggre to Butch as he got close enough to hear without Biggre having to speak too loud. 'And tell your boy to get some too.'

'Hey, watch it. He's my friend.'

'Okay, tell your friend to get some rocks.'

'Hey,' Butch called D and motioned him over. 'We need some stones.'

'Are you nuts. What for?' D replied. 'I'm not messing around in the dirt for nothing. I'm here to get enough money to keep me out of the shit.'

'That's a point. What are we going to do with all these stones?' Butch asked Biggre.

D looked Biggre up and down and condemned him, 'Madman!'

'Mad am I? It's not real. Did you know that? It's not real.'

'What are you talking about?' D asked.

'That's not a proper alarm. No wires.'

'Come off it. Don't you think they can conceal wires.'

'Yes. But those aren't real. They're dummy ones. I got hold of some and sold them myself. It's just a box screwed to the wall. Anyway, have you ever seen a green alarm? We're going to knock it off. Hence the stones.'

'Hence the stones,' echoed Butch, who became a happy man again after being reassured that the sparks was for real.

'Hence the stones,' echoed Derrick, the first to fling a stone into the dud alarm. Ping.

'Wait a minute,' Butch suddenly said. 'If it's a dummy, why are we wasting time knocking it down?'

'For a laugh,' Biggre replied. 'For a laugh.'

Biggre and Derrick joyously stoned the alarm until their hands were empty. Butch stood around scratching his head.

The kicks thudded into the door like a dull tom-tom roll; flat sounding, without much resonance and minimal echo. The door appeared to be giving, then it appeared as though they'd made no impression at all apart from on the paintwork and slight indentations to the wood.

Butch started flagging but the other two were going at it gung-ho. Biggre was a sight, perched on his longer leg and pumping the short one in and out. But then again, we already know that Biggre can kick. D was doing his thing, putting all his energy into it, with vigour and purpose. Too much purpose, perhaps.

Butch stopped to take a breather.

'Come on, it's almost there,' said Biggre.

'Hey, this was your idea. "Once the alarm's done, all you've got to do is barge the door open. Easy as farting," you said. Come on! It'll give soon. Think of all the brown, green and blue bits of paper behind this,' Derrick urged.

Derrick's persuasive effort got Butch back at it, especially the bit about the money.

As soon as Butch said, 'If it doesn't give soon we'll have to leave it.' And Derrick exclaimed, 'What! After all this. You're joking.' The leaf of the double doors which Biggre had hammered at constantly, like a pneumatic drill, flew back.

They hurried through the opening.

## 15

The four of them were seated round a table in *The Hope*.

'He's got money,' said Tommy.

'Fuck off. He aint got shit,' Hangman came in.

'Fuck off yourself. He's got money I said.'

'Stashed in his mattress,' added Paul, giggling. 'Thousands. Enough to set us up sweet.'

'Yeah. Sweet,' confirmed Soulboy, sweetly.

'I aint into robbing tramps. Catch something. Some fucking disease.'

'True,' said Soulboy. 'We'll disinfect the money. Sterilise it.'

'Disinfect. Cleanse. Purify,' said Paul. 'Exterminate. Exterminate,' and laughed.

'So what are we going to do?' asked Soulboy.

'Relieve him of some,' T answered.

'Yeah.' Paul giggled.

'You in, Hangers?' asked T.

'Fuck off,' he replied.

'Fuck off? I'll fuck you. I know what happened, so don't shape with me else I'll walk all over you.'

'My brothers. My brothers. What are we, scavengers?' Soulboy.

'Scavengers. Yeah, scavengers, like them three idiots,' said Paul, still giggling.

They'd got used to it now. The constant giggle. It's only Souls who sometimes still gets freaked by it. It used to get to all of them, now it's just Soulboy.

Tommy Boy loosened up and laughed with or at Paul, so did Souls.

'Are you in, Hangers?' T again asked.

'Didn't I tell you to fuck off.'

'Hey,' and T shoved Hangman's shoulder and stood up sharply. Hangman jumped up too. The clinking glasses and surrounding hub hub faded to complete silence, gradually, yet swiftly. It wasn't a busy night. A few salesmen hung about outside. Say, about twenty people at the most were in the bar. All eyes were on the bad guys.

'Outside or in here?'

'Anywhere you want it,' answered Hangman.

'Hey, you lot over there,' Pete shouted from behind the bar, with the telephone in one hand and the other perched over the dial. 'Any aggro and I'll have the cops down. Now sit down, drink your drinks and try to behave like gentlemen. Or get out.'

Soulboy got up and casually whispered into Tommy's ear, 'You should have let me do him when I had the chance,' then pulled out his hanky, wiped his lips and sat down.

'What's it to be then?' Pete shouted.

'We'll see,' said T to Hangman and sat.

'Yeah,' and Hangman sat down too.

They sat and screwed each other.

Drink your drinks, Pete had said. Soulboy had a fruit juice which he shared with Paul. And that was it. The drinks.

'You in?' Soulboy asked Hangman.

'And you can fuck off, too.'

Hangman immediately grimaced as if overtaken by some great pain.

'What did you say?' Soulboy asked meaningfully, his face right up close to Hangman's. He was right at Hangman's side, their shoulders touching. Soulboy's hand and wrist below table height. His shoulder made a stiff twisting motion and Hangman's face simultaneously became even more taut. Hangman squinted his eyes and bit his lip. 'What did you say?' Soulboy again asked.

'I'm with you. I'm with you. I'm with you,' H replied slavishly.

'Good,' said Soulboy and moved away from Hangers, so now they no longer touch.

'Good. Excellent,' said Paul giggling, naturally.

Hangman clasped both hands around his thigh. The thigh nearest Souls. Soulboy took out a new hanky and wiped his hands. With a sickly sweet sneer on his face he said, 'Get the killer. It's me that gave him the reputation. You know how it is. If a boy wants a rep, you give it to him. Hangman. The only thing he could hang is himself. Get the killer. He couldn't even look. He spewed his guts up.' He looked from Tommy to Hangman in turn as he spoke, slowly turning to face one then the other. Each time he said, 'get the killer' his eyes would be on Hangman and his lip would curl and he'd kiss his teeth as a contemptuous gesture and he'd screw him for a while. Then continue, speaking to T, taking the mick out of H and really putting the verbal knife in. It was Souls who'd killed the guy.

'Exterminate. Exterminate,' Paul piped in. 'Kill. Kill. Mash up,' he was giggling. 'Scavengers,' now he's away. And the whole gang are laughing. Backslapping. Good old boys.

'Are you in?' Soulboy asked politely.

'You know I am,' H replied.

'You know, sometimes I think you've got a screw loose,' said Soulboy affectionately and sounding like he cared. 'A bit of plaster will fix your leg. I'm a pro. Sharp you see. Right in. Right out. A clean cut. Least dangerous of all,' and he put his arm around Hangman and pulled him up close. He threw a sly eye at Paul and whispered in Hangman's ear, 'This parrot's getting to me.'

'Yeah. Me too,' Hangers replied.

After a while Hangman and Tommy's eyes met.

'Cool?' asked T of Hangman.

'Cool.' Hangman replied.


*Praying's for cissies. He took his chances. He isn't afraid of the chair. He was bigtime. Top of the world. Six gun that shoots twenty bullets and all. Hero to the kids on the block. The guy that fought all the way up and isn't afraid of anything. He's eaten at all the best places and had some of the best broads too. Mugging's for the pussies, it's the big stakes that matter. High Rollin'. Repent for what? Wearing the best suits, drinking vintage champagne, smoking the finest Havana cigars and sleeping in the best joints only; Savoy, Ritz, been to them all.*

*He's a bad guy through and through and he's going to be tough through to the end. To the last frizzle when they fry him, he isn't going to cry out,*
*MAMA!*
*'Cos he's soft on his mum. And he would only shed a tear if a*

*priest begged him to, for the children. As an example to the kids.*

*He's a hero to the kids on the block. The guy that fought all the way up and isn't afraid of anything.*


'So, how are we going to do it?' Soulboy asked Tommy.

'Simple. Follow him, get in, then do the business.'

'Just like that?'

'Just like that,' T reaffirmed.

'What about afterwards?'

'What do you mean?'

'Afterwards. He knows us. This is where we live. Every day.'

'You can shut him up, Soulboy,' T replied as if he were over-stating the obvious.

'That's what I thought. It aint worth it to me.'

'I thought you were interested.'

'For a laugh. I was joking. All the hassle for dirty fingernails. It's dirty work, T! I know how we can make richer pickings and all we have to do is stick around and wait and collect. Only babies cosh old Irish drunks on their way home at night. Tut, tut, Tommy Boy, what are we?'

'Scavengers,' said Paul.

And Soulboy muttered to Hangman under his breath, hiss hissing like a viper, 'Do something about that fucking parrot.'

Hangman nodded, yes.


Patrick dropped a clutch of empties which shattered loudly. Instead of looking down, at the broken glass, his gaze shot around the room. Sure enough he'd attracted everyone's attention. A salesman's head came round the part-opened door to see if there was any action.

The salesman flicked a glance at Patrick who stood like the reprimanded child in a full classroom and kissed his teeth, shook his head and withdrew.

'What did I tell you? Not worth it. Waste of time,' Soulboy pronounced to his band.

Paul said, 'Exterminate. Exterminate.'

And Hangman casually slapped him hard across his mouth saying, 'Fucking parrot. Shut it.'

Jenny appeared with a brush, pan and small bin. She gave them to Patrick. 'I'll get something to wipe up with,' she said, went and came back with a squeezy mop. Patrick swept the glass into the pan and emptied it into the bin. Jenny mopped up the booze.

'Are you alright, love?' she asked.

'Yes. I'm fine. An accident that's all.'

'Are you sure?'

'Yes. I'm fine.'

'Well, I've spoken to Pete. He's agreed that since you opened up for us today you can leave early.'

'To do what?'

'Have an early night,' she suggested.

'I'm an insomniac.'

'You're a crackpot. Have an hour off. Leave at ten.'

'Ay ay cap'n.'

'So, are you going to empty that bin or stand around posing with it all night?'

'Give me the mop, I'll put that away too.'

She gave it to him and he went to empty the glass in the big bin out back.


'Hey,' T called. Patrick carried on wiping an unoccupied table, two away from where those bad boys are.

'Hey,' T called again. Pete stopped and looked over.

'I'm talking to you!' T shouted at Patrick. Patrick looked at T.

For an instant it was as if the hours between opening up and now had never happened. It was as if Patrick had closed the door and heard them drive off, then turned to find the pub as it is at the moment. Anywhichway he turned, Patrick could not escape T Boy's eyes.

'There's a table to be cleared.' Tommy Boy pointed at the empty fruit juice bottle.

'No rush,' Patrick replied.

'I'm a customer and I want my table cleared.' T thumped the table in mock indignation.

'One bottle?' asked Patrick.

'I want to speak to the manager.'

'Clear it,' Pete shouted over. Patrick hesitated. 'Go on,' Pete urged.

'Come and clear my table,' said T to a frozen Patrick. 'Come, come. I'm a regular here. Never cause any trouble. Always polite. Pay good money. And I can't get my table cleared. You want to employ some decent bar staff, mate,' he said to Pete.

Pete opened the hatch in the bar and Rusty came bounding out. The Policeman.

'I don't give a shit about the dog. You've been watching too many old films, mate. Chain gang and shit. Blacks shit it if you've got a good dog and all that. I'll kill it,' said Soulboy, poker faced and looking good. Soulboy's got a wicked alsatian. A bitch with a mean tendency. If you stick your hand out above her she goes for it, natural, always done it, since she was a puppy. A mother.

Jenny must have let Rusty in because there she is, standing there watching things with him. She disappeared when Tommy first started up. She wasn't with Pete a minute ago.

'Get the bottle,' said Pete. Rusty went upside Patrick and escorted him to and away from the table.

Soulboy got up to leave. 'Let's go,' he said, and the gang got up and left. There was a red patch on one of Hangman's trouser legs. Small red specks swam downstream of the patch. Red dots marked his trail from the table to the door.

Butch tugged the pull switch dangling from the ceiling and the floor lit up. The rails were there but they were bare. The sewing machines were all cramped together in a corner of the factory floor. The presses were unhitched from the steam supplies and bundled together. Some of the presses and machines were tied in pairs. Odd shaped strips of unredeemable lining material and tangled heaps of thread were all about; on the floor; on the bundled machinery; in between and around company brochures, pamphlets like tracts and catalogues that covered the floor and up the wooden staircase to the office or what was the office, like matting; everywhere, liberally.

Biggre looked at Butch and said, 'You owe me five grand. And hassle money for getting the wheels.'

'They were here last Friday. I saw them loading gear. I checked.' Butch scratched his head. 'The coats they make here cost thousands.'

'Made,' said Biggre. 'Past tense.'

Butch walked over to the machines and started searching between them. 'Ten coats and I could have booked my flight.'

Derrick picked through some of the catalogues. 'Where are the offices?'

'Upstairs,' Butch replied.

'Have they got a safe?'

'Aha,' Butch raised his eyebrows. 'Yes they have.'

Like automatons reprogrammed, their collective attention turned to the office at the top of the stairs. Without a word they headed for the safe.

'Be cool. You'll get your money,' said Butch to Biggre as he stood on the bottom rung with Biggre ahead of him.

Biggre stopped, without turning he asked, 'Can you open safes? Or are we going to kick open a three inch thick steel door?'

'Why not? Anything for a laugh, eh, Butch,' D said.

'No names,' said Biggre.

Derrick, who was ahead of them both and going through the

office door, didn't respond. The other two lagged behind saying things he couldn't hear.

They're all in the office and it's like downstairs. There are no chairs, no desks, no coat stand or clock.

A bedevilled Derrick is sitting beside the telephone (one of the few things left behind). His back is up against the wall, whole sole on the floor and knees up. He picks up the receiver. He waits for the dialling tone. No dialling tone. It's a bad day for Derrick and phones. He starts to dismantle it, undoing screws with the little penknife on his key-ring. A harmless thing. A while ago I would have said the penknife was DERRICK'S penknife. It summed him up. Believe me. The cover that goes over the dial is off. He's taking the bell off. It's off. He's prodding the circuit board. Now he's at the receiver. Crash. He's thrown it against the wall and his head drops between his knees, his hands go up and cup his head. His forearms press against his ears and his elbows come in around his stomach. 'Shit, how I need you now, Naomi,' he thought. Naomi, the solace at the end of the line, now that we are at the end of the line. There's no way out. 'Next time I'm going to kill you,' he thought and the voice of his thought was Hangman's. In effect, Hangman had been threatening D all day.

There are no pictures on the wall. No unused order books or forgotten picture of the wife or the kids or the two in tandem, captured as a group. There is no safe.

'Your bag,' Biggre said sharply. D was on another planet. 'Your bag,' Biggre said again. Derrick's head came up. His eyes were red and tearful and angry. Butch and Biggre looked at their pal with concern. Derrick's face expressed too much sadness.

'Your bag. If anyone sees it, we've had it. There isn't any point in getting done for nothing, now is there? Pull yourself together, mate,' Biggre's voice was full of gentleness and earnest compassion. So full, so deep, that Butch had to turn and smile and ask, 'What next?'

Biggre smiled and Derrick went.

'Woman?' Biggre asked.

'Don't know,' Butch replied.

'Only a woman could do that to a man.'

'What makes you say that?'

'I'm not saying anything. Did you get it?'

'Get what?'

'Joanne?'

'What's it to you?' Butch asked.

'You worked here?' Biggre asked.

'For a while. What is it with you and her anyway?' Butch tried to subtly draw Biggre.

'What did you do here?' He was having none of it.

'Try and survive.'

'Hard?'

'It was alright. Jewish people. Up and down, you know. Don't know where they're coming from. Cool but unpredictable. Some days would be a laugh. I couldn't live on the money. I used to come in when they had work. No cards and stuff. The money was irregular and never that great. I was going through one of those phases. Looking for steady work and things. I wasn't casing the place or anything. It was a straight up job.'

'Straight up?'

'Yes. Straight up. I used to stamp the sizes and styles on tickets and pin them to the coats. And when the carriers came, put the coats in batches and load them up.'

'Very interesting. So I'm here for nothing then? I don't believe it. There's got to be something in this.'

'Follow,' Butch commanded. He led Biggre into the women's loo.

'Phew, what a reek. When you think of women, all pure and gentle and sweet like.'

'Motherly,' Butch interjected.

'Yeah, motherly. You wouldn't dream that their insides could be so smelly.'

'Don't talk rubbish.' Butch was on his knees and pulling back the lino under the washbasin.

Biggre is leaning against the wall looking relaxed but attentive. 'Have you ever imagined Joan Collins having a shit. Or Di or one of those slinky model types in the Duran videos. A well stink runny shit, splattering the bowl and smelling like rotten fruit. Everyone's done one at some time or the other. It must be shattering to capture a hot thing, take her back to base and she lets off a right rich raspberry, leaving a skid as long as your arm in her baggies.'

'You're sick.' Butch ripped up a floorboard with ease and dug up a small cash box.

Biggre saw. 'Knew it,' he said.

'Contingency measures.'

'Plan B?'

'Naturally.'

'So what's the form?' Biggre asked, his face lighting up.

'Five hundred quid.'

'Straight up?'

'Straight up.'

'Not the money. The work?'

'It was. I told you, it was a really nice place to work. Only one thing ever reached me. They couldn't find the petty cash once. They asked me if I knew where it was about a dozen times. It turned up. I don't know how but they found it. It went missing in the morning and they found it in the afternoon.'

Biggre pointed at the box in Butch's hand. 'Open it.'

'What with?' Butch stood up. 'We'll open it in the car.'

'Are you going to walk down the street cradling it in your arms. Don't be stupid.'

'Okay, okay. Where's D?'

'No names.'

'Where is he?'

'He'll be back, he's not a baby, you know. So they thought you nicked it?'

'Of course. They asked me from the time I got in right up to lunch. It was in their eyes too. I could read them,' Butch said as he walked out the bog, to the stairs and scanned the shop floor for sight of his mate. Nothing.

'So you decided to mete out a little poetic justice.' Biggre now standing in the office doorway.

'Of course.'

'The irony of it.'

'Yeah,' and Butch turned to see Biggre wearing horn-rimmed glasses, a crisp clean white shirt and slacks. There's a trick to this. Butch, agog, simply beseeched, 'How?'

'Pardon?'

Derrick came in with his bag. He looked worn.

'Come on, man,' called Butch.

'Hey, Butch, don't push me,' D called back.

'How come your friend's such a rank amateur?' Biggre asked.

'There's nothing wrong with being a useless thief. He's not like you and me.'

'How come he's your friend then? You two are always together.'

'So, we're always together. So what. All my friends aren't thieves. I should have left him out.'

'Too late now, my friend.'

'I don't need it, Biggre.'

'No names.'

'Piss off.'

Derrick reached them. 'Got the mallet?' Butch asked. And D whipped it out.

Derrick saw the box. 'Nice one. Where was it?'

'Contingency measures,' Butch replied.

'Plan B,' added Biggre.

'Where have you been all this time?' Butch asked.

'Mind your own business and open the box.'

'Steady yourself, D.'

'I've told you before, Butch, I don't need steadying.'

Biggre said, 'The whole world knows we're here now. The

operation's gone haywire,' and walked out to sit on the stairs.

'You open it,' said Butch to Derrick, handing him back the mallet. 'If the hammer can't do it, rip it off with your teeth, Conan.'

D smashed the box open quickly, efficiently and with plenty of gusto. And enough noise too. Outside, on the steps, Biggre groaned. Under his breath he called the two of them all the names under the sun, with the exception of their real ones. True Pro's. Real Stars. Men From Nowhere With No Names. That's how it should be. Like it is in the flicks. Those two are pulling the blag apart at the seams.

'It's done,' shouted D.

Biggre stood up. 'Give me my money and let me get out of here.'

Butch pointed out that he was their driver.

'Alright, split it up and I'll go and get the car. Come on. How much did you say it was? Do you want me to count it?'

'Five hundred.'

'Nice.'

'I'll split it up,' D volunteered. And got on with it before the other two had a chance to say yes or no.

Butch told Derrick that it wouldn't take them to LA but it was something.

'Something like what, Butch. Like what?' his buddy replied.

Biggre asked what they were talking about.

## 17

Joanne had been home and washed and scrubbed up and changed and was on her way back to Butch's place. She wore a denim jacket and jeans, a tee shirt and inappropriate shoes for an intermittently drizzly evening; sandals. One of the jacket sleeves came away at the shoulder slightly — the stitching was coming undone — and was held in place by a small gold-coloured pin. Nice. She carried an overnight bag. Heads turn as she passes. She says 'Hi' to two old dears talking over the wall at the front of their homes. Her red hair, resplendent and bouncy, exemplifies the vibes she's giving off.

It's some walk from her home to the estate. The route takes her past the town hall and the park. She walked straight past her lover without knowing it.

Butch told her that he'd be at the flat around nine. I think Derrick had just drawn his mallet around that time. It's about nine o'clock. She'd already decided to let herself in if Butch isn't there when she arrives. The trick with the cardboard's easy.

From time to time her walking pace would increase, speed up. It would be as if she wanted to run but was somehow being restrained. Just when it seemed she was about to slip anchor and take off full speed ahead, her tempo would come down. The increases in her step would be matched by an equal increase in the look of urgent excitement on her face. She bubbled like sparkling wine; fizzing, crackling and popping and set to blow the cork away at any time. Self-control takes her back down to the ground and earths her.

A guy that's seen her around recognises her as he passes by and says 'Hi'. He stopped, wanting to talk but can't find the right line quick enough. He's a cool guy who's never failed to get off base before. The thing is, he's never given a second's consideration to talking to Joanne before either. He's a lot like Butch and D and all the other dudes really. They only talk to her for a laugh and in groups, where they can impress one another by taking the piss out of her. But to her, there's something about Butchy Baby. She said 'Hi' back to the guy and carried on about her business as if he were transparent. Her thoughts were elsewhere. That's one ego at base point hobbling around somewhere.

She told her mum, 'He's not like the others. He really cares about me.'
And her mother replied, 'Why don't you stop looking for a man to care about you and start caring for yourself. They're only after one thing.'
'Tell me about it, mum. There isn't exactly a queue of eligible honourable types badgering me for my thing.'
'Eligible? Honourable? Do me a favour. Men like that want virgins and only virgins, or as near as damn it.'
'I'm well out of the running.'
'Don't I know it. What's his name?'
'Butch.'
'Butch?'
'William Butcher.'
'Nice. It's got a ring to it.'
'He's a good guy, mum.'
'Black?'
'Yes.'
'Well, no point talking to you about that, is there?'
'No. This is the twentieth century. We've gone beyond all that.'
'Some of us, not all. You just watch yourself.'
'Butch knows all the angles, mum. All the angles. He'll see I'm alright.'
'Jack the lad. Don't you think you'd be better off taking a girlfriend?'
'It's what I want.'
'Butch?' Joanne's mum mused over the name.
'That's his name.'

'She might not want to put you up if you've got a boy with you?'

'We'll manage. Getting there is the hard bit, the rest is easy. LA, mum, where it all happens.'

'Maybe this isn't such a good idea after all.'

'I'm not a schoolgirl. It's an opportunity I can't afford to miss out on. What's here for me? Nothing. I can get any seat for the next two weeks. Everything's booked. She said I could bring a friend for the first three weeks, so I'm going to do just that. Anyway, I promised him.'

'How could you have promised him anything? You never knew it was booked until I told you when you came in.'

'Come off it, mum. We've been expecting it for ages. She said she would, and she always keeps her word.'

'I think you're too young for this. I'd better ring her and explain.'

'If you do, I'll leave anyway.'

'Sleep on it. Think about it some more.'

'I want to go. It's the chance of a lifetime. You were dead keen until I told you about him. You can't run my life for me. I'm not doing it to hurt you.'

'I guess you've made your mind up.'

'I have.'

'You will at least try and spend the weekdays here, won't you. I don't know what I'm getting so worked up about. I hardly see you anyway. And when I do you're like the living dead.'

'Thank you very much.'

'So, are you going to be around? See your dad before you go? When do you think you'll be leaving? I ought to shoot my sister for encouraging you. You're just like her. Remember, people who are too much alike can't get on for very long.'

'Me and her have always got on, always will.'

'You're probably right. So, when are you going over? I'll see you off if you like, meet Mr Butcher.'

'Now or sooner, mum. I just want to go.'

'Without seeing your friends, your cousins?'

'My father? What's the point? That would be real hypocrisy. I've told YOU and that's enough. I can come back and see you in three weeks, then go out again if I still like it. I'll write you. I'll phone.'

'And your aunt will pay. She fleeces that man for every penny, you know. The two of you will bankrupt him.'

'He's loaded. I bet the flights are on his expense account. Her Walter sounds smart.'

'Like Butch.'

'In a way. They both know how to keep their heads above water.'

'And is that all there is to it?'

'What more can you ask for? One day you're up, the next you're down, and then up and then down again, and so on and so on. Isn't that the way it is everywhere? Only thing is, in LA up means way up.'

'And down means down and out?'

'Down is down anywhere. In LA there's a bottom like anywhere else, but there's no top. You can go as high as you want.'

'Do you believe that?'

'It's the only way to fly. Today I've got a man and a start somewhere else. In one day. Wouldn't you have taken it, mum?'

'What will I do without you?' and her mum burst into tears. 'You look radiant,' she said.


She reached the spot where Butch had simply said, 'Home.' She thought about it and said, 'Cute.' She said, 'Digress,' and laughed out loud. Good thing there weren't many people about. They'd have thought she was nutty. She had trouble controlling her laughter because the word kept going round and round her head, getting funnier and funnier all the time. Her pace had picked up too.

Eventually she appeared at the steps leading to the penthouse, as he called it. At the mouth of the stairwell, the smell of her perfume mingled with the pungent trash momentarily. She covered her nose and skipped spritely up the stairs.

She did the lock, went in and fell into the cushions laughing freely.

# Afterwards

## 18

They were leaving casually; looking about as they made their way to the door. Biggre stopped and said he'd heard something. Butch called him paranoid and over-anxious. He said, 'We've been here almost three-quarters of an hour, if someone had been snooping around we'd have known.'

'It's a voice. Did you hear that?' Biggre asked.

There was a low moan coming from the direction of the sewing machines. Derrick came in with an emphatic 'I didn't hear anything' brusquely, and carried on to the door.

Butch and Biggre were rooted. They froze, staring at the machines. Then the moan sounded again and there was visible movement amongst the pile.

'What have you done?' Butch shouted to Derrick who was now out the door and out of sight.

Biggre wanted to follow D's example. 'Let's get out of here. Derrick did it and he's off, so what are we hanging around for?'

'What's he done?' Butch asked himself.

'You're pushing your luck. Let's get out of here.'

Butch started slowly walking over to the machines. He hadn't taken his eyes off them since the first audible moan. The machines had been moved about. He noticed that one bundle of machines — which was barely visible under masses of scattered thread when they first came in — was leant up against another bundle at an angle and most of the thread had slipped off. He had avoided that bundle when he clambered over the machines searching for forgotten coats. 'What's he done?' he thought.

Biggre grabbed Butch's arm. 'Leave it. Leave it.'

'I've got to see.' He pulled his arm free.

'Why man? Why?'

'Look, go if you want to.'

'And I thought you were smart.'

Butch's eyes caught the man lying on the floor on his stomach, his forehead propped on a pedal. When the man left for work this morning he was probably well dressed. He probably has an average amount of children and is into his second marriage. He is in his late thirties, early forties. He wore brogues; brown brogues with those really thick soles and dusty with dirt, pebbles and sand maybe. Shoes that the stuffy, prim, square jawed, bewhiskered old major ranting about the last days of raj as he warms his backside by an open fire — tweed jacket, leather trim and elbow patches, port in hand — in the cottage that's been in the family for years, would wear. The man's suit was crumpled, however, more up-to-date. Modern. An appropriate suit for his age. He had dark hair.

'Don't touch him!'

Butch sucked his teeth. 'What do you take me for?' The man's eyelids fluttered. 'Are you alright, mate?' he asked.

Biggre slid out of the man's line of vision slickly. 'Do what you like. I don't want him picking me out of a line up.'

'Not a chance. You're never the same for five minutes.'

'Tell him all about me.' The man moaned and tried to raise his head. 'Some people have been sussed by having their voice identified.'

'You'd better shut up then, Biggre.'

'No names. No names.' And Biggre moved even further away. Then D came back in. 'Where's the car, Biggre?'

'I'm not giving out any more info. You'll have to work it out.'

'What's wrong with this man?' D asked Butch.

'Which one?'

'Are you cutting me out, Butch?'

'Of what?'

76

'Why all this double talk?'

'This one,' and Butch pointed at the man. 'Or that one,' then at Biggre.

Derrick couldn't see the man between the machines from where he stood. He assumed it was another of his mate's unfathomable jokes and let it pass. He swung his thumb in the direction of Biggre. 'This idiot.'

'How can you call anyone an idiot?' asked Biggre. 'Walk towards the park. You can't miss it. I'll wait for five minutes.'

'Why can't he say what motor he's got? Is that anything?' D asked Butch.

Biggre said, 'It's blue,' and split.

'What are you hanging on for, Butch? Christmas. Come on, let's go.'

'Did you have to?'

'Have to what?'

'Don't pretend. What's this?' Butch showed him the machinery.

'What?' D hadn't moved and still couldn't see.

'You're going on like one of those funny people. Like a psycho. Like one of those people who blank out anything they can't deal with.'

'I know everything I've done. What are you on about? You think you know everything. And when did you become a psychiatrist. If you were that good, you wouldn't be here.'

The man moaned and Butch looked at Derrick. 'Did you hear that? I don't need a psychiatrist to understand that.'

'Leave it. I didn't hear anything.'

'So, why did you do it?'

'I didn't do anything.'

'Come and look at him then.'

'Why?'

'You can't do it. That's what you get for acting the hard man. You've gone too far this time, Derrick.'

'Stuff it, Butch, I'll look at him. I hope you know he'll be able to recognise us after this.'

Derrick went up close to the man. The man's head rose straight up and his eyes shot open for an instant. A stream of vomit belched out of his mouth. D ducked out of the way and the man's cannoned innards just missed him. D looked up at Butch and said, 'The things I do for you.' The man moaned with substance; a recuperative moan. He mumbled sounding like, 'Leave me alone. Let me sleep. Let me sleep.' Whatever it was, the man made it plain that they were gate-crashing his little scene.

'Pissed,' D pronounced. 'This is a pissed man. Can we go now. Biggre isn't going to wait forever.'

'What was I supposed to think. It's the way you've been acting.'

'Acting? I'm not acting, Butch.'

## 19

They could see Biggre from way up the alley. He was perched on the bonnet with his arms folded across his chest.

'It's red,' Derrick exclaimed.

'Look for any car but a blue one is what he meant,' Butch replied.

D should surely know better by now. Biggre is a flash devil.

'Is he alright. He hasn't turned fool has he?'

'No. Of course he's alright.'

'Well at least he hasn't changed again. How does he do it, Butch?'

'Search me.'

'No need. How much have you got?'

'A bit.'

'Enough to build one up?'

'In the car?'

'Yeah. Why not?'

'What's all this. You don't smoke.'

'Build one,' D ordered.

'You sure?'

'Stop checking me.'

'Alright, alright. I'll build it if you'll smoke it?'

'I'll smoke. And I'm sure he's cracked. Did you find out about him and the woman?'

'What do you mean?'

'Did you ask him about Joanne?'

'What's there to ask. And didn't I tell you to keep your nose out.'

'Not in those very words. No.'

'Well I have now, haven't I?'

'Roger, over and out.'

'It's pretty powerful.' Butch back on le erb.

'The stronger the better.'

'Hold up, Tiger.'

'Just one puff,' D said.

'Are you cool now? You had me worried for a while there.'

'I'm cool, Butch.'

'Let people like Hangman deal with their own. They're cutters, man. Guys walking around trying to kill one another, when it's hard enough getting from one end of the day to the other. They need education. You think Biggre's crazy? It's all about building, D. Catch Biggre on a good day and talk to him. He's no idiot. He's like the paddy man, when you talk to them they can tell you about all sorts of things.'

'Drunks and madmen. No thanks.'

'You prefer killers? Hangman and them are the way they are because of things they don't know. They need to learn certain things.'

'I know, Butch, they need a lesson.'

'Weren't you listening to me?'

'Get off the soap box, man. I've got my own mind. You think you're so smart. Shut it!'

'It's your arse I'm thinking about.'

'Thanks, but I can look after it for myself. Thanks but no thanks, if you get what I mean.'

Butch stopped and stood up to his mate. 'So what are you going to do if I don't? Kill me. Smash my skull with your hammer.'

'Move out of my way, Butch.'

Biggre saw them standing there, up the road from the car parked outside the town hall. He jumped off the bonnet and stood arms akimbo shooting daggers at them with his eyes. 'What is this?' he muttered. 'Never again! These guys are cop fodder.' He went into his petulant dance; his upper lip almost touching his nose; ahuffing and apuffing; kicking the ground and going up and down pneumaticlike.

'What are you going to do, D? All day you've been like this. Man! How can I be around you if I've got to watch every little word?'

'Little word, my arse. Get out of my way, man.'

'My name's Butch. Mister Butcher, if you really want to get formal. What is this? If you're going to do me, do me now. I'm with you all the time. You're bound to do it sometime at this rate. So do it now. Do it now, D.'

'Get out of my way, Butch.'

'How do you get out of the inevitable, D?' Butch asked in a calmer voice than anything else he'd previously said. 'How? I won't stop until we've worked it out. I'm not afraid of you. I'm not going to stand around and watch you turn into mess like me. I haven't got anything I haven't had to get for myself. I've got to like looking out for myself because I haven't got any choice. Soulboy and them are more my scene. They're not for you.'

'You, handle them? They terrorise you, Butch. Them boys are plain raht naht hooligans.'

'They terrorise me? I'm not afraid of them.'

'You're a good actor then. You should have a handful of Oscars for the performances I've seen you give when they're around.'

'You're not handling it right. The trick is in being able to stay cool. Never let them get you going up the wall. Stay loose. Look, go home, give your mother some sweet words, get some food in your belly and rest up. Take what's yours. I wish I was in your place. Take it easy, D. Don't give yourself such a hard time. It's the advice of a true friend.'

'Alright, alright.' Derrick cooled off and walked around Butch. Butch turned to follow him, his face well sanctimonious and self-satisfied; Freud, you know. They both suddenly stopped. 'Okay,' D said. 'Explain this to me. Explain this and I'll say you know something.'

'He's cool but he's something else.'

'Is that an answer? Are we going to get in a car with that? It's going to drive I suppose?'

'He's cool.'

'I preferred your first answer.'

'Let's go, this place is getting to be a bore.'

Derrick laughed.

Biggre leant against the motor, reading, wearing robes of red, green and gold once more.

As Butch and Derrick settled in their seats, Biggre turned the ignition key and said, 'My brothers. My brothers.'

And Derrick asked him straight out, 'Are you on the level?'

'Are you?'

D told Butch to skin up. Butch skilfully obliged. D took the one puff. 'I don't feel anything. That stuff's got no effect on me.'

'Well, what do you expect?' Butch asked. 'It's just a bit of weed, not coke or anything. Here,' and he shoved the joint back.

'No. I'll have a drink instead. Are we going to the pub?'

'No. I've got to get back,' Butch replied.

'Aha,' said Derrick.

'Aha what? You can come and watch if you like?'

'No thanks.'

Biggre unexpectedly volunteered to go with Derrick and took the spliff from Butch. 'Cool.'

'You don't drink,' D said.

'Watch me.'

*The car takes a directionless course through the backstreets, sometimes straight and under control, sometimes veering to the left or right — only slightly, but veering nonetheless. The sky is angry and weeps continuously. The man behind the wheel is enveloped by his clothing. A hat with its brim pulled down to just above eye level; jacket with upturned lapels. The wipers slash hopelessly at the water raining down the windscreen.*

*Let's go inside. Let's get inside the car beside the man. Let's go right inside.*

*Every now and again he grimaces and grips the steering wheel tight. Beads of perspiration have made a soaked sponge of his face. Every pore is open and gushing. His red leering eyes are on edge and ready to run for it. They look ready to bail out of their sockets.*

*Pearly droplets of blood dribble down his sleeve and land on his leg. Sirens wail out in the night serving notice of pursuance. The sweeping, swirling, whirling, whooping wail gets closer and closer. His eyes shoot this way and that in search of an illusive nest to which he can retreat and hold up 'til the heat cools off. He curses his luck and the guy who split on the gang. Snitch!*

*He can't believe his eyes. An opening in a familiar wall. An opening that he can't recall having seen before. He leans forward and stares anxiously through the waterfall of a windscreen; with a smile, he drives full speed into the opening.*

'Slow down, Biggre.' Biggre's driving put Butch on edge.

'It's alright, man,' Biggre replied.

'Leave him alone, Butch. The man's cool, remember. Anyway, I like it fast.'

'We're flying, my brother. Flying,' Biggre sang.

'Yeah, Butch. We're flying. We're flying.'

'It's infectious,' Butch declared.

'Yes and you should catch some,' D proposed.

'Truly,' and Biggre seconded. 'Can I drop you off on the road? It's too much hassle going round and round the court-yard.'

'Yes.'

Biggre stopped the car before the driveway taking you through the arch and into the courtyard. Butch bundled out and took a huge gulp of air and shook his head to steady himself. 'Whew!' I should know better than to smoke that stuff in cars. It's murderous when the air hits you. See you later, Biggre. Come up later if you like, Derrick.'

'Don't you want me in your home,' Biggre asked. 'Aren't you inviting me?'

'Of course. There's a first time for everything.'

'The motto of a barbarian. See you around, Butch.'

Derrick broke his silence and laughed.

'Are you alright now, D?'

'Yeah, yeah.'

'Are we going to see you later?'

'We?'

'Are you going to come up? We'll go out somewhere. We've got the money for once.'

'I can look after myself, man. There's no need to worry, I told you.'

Biggre told Butch that Derrick was a man. Butch persisted and asked if he wanted to go to the penthouse now.

D said, 'Come on. Let's go,' to Biggre. And Biggre started up. D said, 'See you, Butch.'

'Keep cool, D.'

'I'm cool,' D replied as the car moved off.

'He's cool,' Biggre confirmed. All of a sudden the car was too far down the road to converse without yelling.

'I should have gone with him,' Butch thought. 'Well at least I know where he is. I can always slip out and see what he's up to.'

# Night-time

## 20

Butch flew up the steps and was standing in the hallway of his flat quicker than you could snap your fingers.

Immediately, his eyes settled on Joanne standing in the centre of the front room directly under the light (shaded, so dimmed) and looking lovelier than she'd ever looked.

He was oblivious to everything except her.

So as not to seem too eager or keen or pussy-struck he played for time. He had to act cool. You know, no big deal.

'Where's Joanne?' he asked out loud to himself; looking around, making out like he couldn't see her, making her smile because it was too too obvious that he could. He popped his head around the kitchen door, bedroom door and bog, calling out her name. 'I know you're here somewhere,' he'd say. She didn't respond so he just carried on mucking around. He finally, despairingly, had no alternative but to declare his love short but sweet as he trudged back into the front room.

'Is it sweet, Butch?' she asked.

'Oh, it's you,' he replied.

'Stop messing about. Be serious.'

'You look nice,' he said, putting his arms around her waist and drawing her in close and cutting out the playacting.

'Nice?' and she pushed him away.

'Yes, nice. Really nice,' and he drew her back in.

They made it without another word passing between them.

Afterwards, she asked him, 'Where did you go to tonight?'

'No shackles.'

'It's not a shackle, it's a question,' and she squeezed his balls. He pretendingly doubled up in agony, grunting and groaning in pain.

'I'll talk. I'll talk. I'll talk. I'll tell you everything you want to know, only please don't squeeze my balls again,' he gushed and opened his legs invitingly and positioning himself so that she could get at them easily.

She put her hand over his genitals; close to and hovering around, but not touching. Close enough for Butch to feel the heat. 'Now talk,' she said. 'Where were you on the night of such and such with a Mister D?' She paused for a bit. 'I don't know his surname.'

'Massive.'

'A Mister D Matthews?'

Butch laughed to himself. 'On business.'

'Could we try and be more explicit, Mister Butcher. What sort of business?'

He felt her lowered hand just about touching him. 'Good business, and I've been paid.'

'Makes sense.' And her hand moved gently across and up and down inside his thighs. Then they started to kiss and finally fell into one another for a second time.

They were at the point where the mind and body float. The point where the tongue runs freely and the mind ambles. The point where there aren't any more bright sparks or high fliers. That hallowed time just after. Magic seconds. Feeling good with somebody. Laying spread eagle out from under the sheets. Open. Opened eyes aware of only a great expanse about. No walls. No boundaries. The stars zoom around the ceiling. The universe, contained here in this room. Just the two of them, Butch and Jo. And it seemed so right and blissful and wow, making love can be great when you're on top of the world.

'So, how much did you get for your labours?'

'Enough.'

'Enough? Can't you open up for once?'

'Okay. I got one hundred and sixty-six sixty-eight, because I sussed the job out. D and the other guy got one hundred and sixty-six sixty-six pence. Satisfied your curiosity?'

'Was it hard work?'

'Yes. Well hard.'

'My poor baby.' She took his hands and looked at them, palms up, checking for signs of the wear and tear of manful labours. She lightly rubbed and blew on them to soothe. 'You're going to make a great provider. You're like a sweet little bird with a puffed out breast, perched ever so lightly on a delicate twig, alert and looking over his chicks nesting on branches below. You're so sweet, Butch. Will you go out and work for me every day, come rain or shine?'

'Are you kidding?'

'Come home to the wife and kids, dinner in the oven.'

'Bun in the oven.'

'It's going to be sweet, Butch. But first we're going to have to go somewhere where there isn't any prejudice. It would upset my mum to think that I lived somewhere dangerous.'

'I don't fancy the outer Himalayas.'

'So, nothing's perfect. Just somewhere better than here.'

'It's the same everywhere. And I'm not ready for children.'

'I can wait.'

'And you can be very strange. I'm not working for anyone.'

'William Butcher, a man's man.'

He got sharp. 'I'm not that kind of person. I'll do what I can for people I care about. Which reminds me, what's the time? I've got to find Derrick.'

'Look at your watch.'

'Half eleven. I've got to go.'

'He's not a baby. Ease off. Derrick's got more know-how than you have.'

'You think so?'

'Yes.'

'So do I. It's just today. It's been a funny day.'

'For all of us, including me. Don't forget me. We're going, Butch.' He didn't reply. 'I said we're going.'

'Going where? If I'm going anywhere, it's to look up D.'

'We're going to LA.'

'I think I'll go round his house. Annoy his mum. If I take a cab I'll be back before you know I've gone. Want to come?'

'I already have, several times. Butch, we're going to LA.'

'By pedal steamer?'

'No. Big white bird.'

'When do we go?'

'Now if you like.'

Butch was up and putting his clothes on. He'd turned his back to her. The turn-up in his trouser wouldn't stay up. He wrestled with it.

'Do I have to show you the tickets to get you to believe me?' she thought.

His tone became patronising. 'Okay. You don't mind if we go and tell D, do you? I mean, from his place to Gatwick's no problem.'

'Heathrow actually.'

'I'm not sure about you staying around here, Joanne. Maybe we're just getting carried away. The heat and everything. Maybe it's because I'm not getting enough. I'll drop you off. Are you going home?' He was fully dressed, picking up the cushions and shaking them back to life. She didn't move, so he could only get at some of them. In fact, she stretched out and positioned herself in such a way that her small frame seemed to somehowortheother be in contact with most of the cushions. Old neat and tidy Butch. Mister Cleanliness Itself. She knew she was getting to him, so she didn't even flinch an inch to let him get on with his tidying up.

'Do you want me to go now?' she teased.

'You're weird. Don't take it all so seriously. LA, it's a dream. A way of letting off steam. A good joke to keep us going, that's all. How many more times are you going to turn weird on me? It's like this afternoon.'

'What about this afternoon? You mean, sleeping with Biggre. When you dropped the glass.' She started laughing uncontrollably, pointing at Butch's pouting, disapproving expression every now and again to stoke the embers of her amusement to a flame over and over.

Butch stood there shaking his head. He'd intermittently say 'You're weird' to her.

'Joanne, I'm in a hurry.'

'Don't you want to go? Can't you hear what I'm saying?'

'Yeah, I can hear you. Can you hear me? Can you hear what I'm saying? Watch my lips; joke over!'

'No LA?'

'No nothing!'

'Are you for sale, Butch?'

'For sale? Are you getting up or aren't you? I've got to go.'

'Not yet. Have you got a price, I said?'

Butch gave up and sat beside the stereo. He pulled a record from a tatty sleeve and put it on. The artist girl had left it behind. It was old and hissed, but the sax was nice. Lynne Hope playing 'tenderly' and stuff. Sixties music. It can soothe you. Good music for early hours.

She said, 'If only you knew Biggre. You don't know how quick he can change. He came out of the bedroom like a different person. I don't know how, but Damon — that's their little boy.'

'I know. Cute.'

'Yes. He went to sleep not long after I walked out. And then Biggre came out and started talking to me real calm. He made me coffee. Cup and saucer. The complete gentleman. It's not every day I meet a gentleman who says he loves me like he means it. And that's what he did, Butch. He said it with his mouth, eyes and everything.'

'So you slept with him just like that?'

'Yes. I couldn't help it. At the time it was irresistible.'

'Fantastic!'

'Has it never happened to you?'

He didn't answer, so she answered for him, 'Of course it has. And it's happened to me again, today. I think it happened to you too. I want to stay with you, Butch. Don't you want to stay with me? Anyway, you don't know Biggre, he can turn just like that,' she snapped her fingers.

'I get the point.'

'He's never been the same since. He's an awkward bastard.'

'Language.'

'I'll never be a lady.'

'They're the biggest tramps of all.'

'So it's okay for me to swear but not okay for me to be a tramp?'

'Neither.'

'Fine, fine. Are we going to LA?'

'Now this frightens me. Is it a fixation?'

'No. It's real. I want you to believe me. I've squared with you on Biggre, why should I mess around now?'

'Alright. Show me the tickets. You haven't got them on you. We'll pick them up on the way, right?'

'Wrong.'

'Show me them then.'

'Are you for sale, Butch?'

'Yes.'

She reached over, picked up the phone and booked the flight, quoting all the bumph her aunt told her to. 'Do you think we'll get there in time?' she asked.

Butch was stunned to silence.

'Aren't you excited?' she asked.

'Excited?' He flew over to Joanne and hugging and kissing and tickling rolled all over the room with her, entangled in the sheet that part covered them for a while, when they first went to bed earlier in the evening.

## 21

It is as they were when they drove up to the pub in the early afternoon. Tommy Boy drove, Soulboy sat beside him, Paul and Hangman were in the back; Paul behind Soulboy and Hangers behind T. Paul was sleeping soundly. He snored. A swift sharp elbow to the ribs, delivered by the guy seated next to him on instruction from the smooth one seated up front, soon put paid to that.

T checked the petrol gauge. It was low. He drove into the first garage he came across, got out and went to fill up with four star. The nozzle came out of its holster easy enough but it didn't seem to want to go back. It kept slipping out. The first time it slipped, the rubber hose projected the nozzle and flung oil at him. He dodged the oil like a matador, nice and fancy, good footwork and under control. Soulboy saw it and Hangers did too. They nodded self-gratuitous approval to each other and posed for a time. However, when T tried to put the nozzle back a second time and it jumped out again, he looked over to his muckers with an ironic smile and they simply looked away and engrossed themselves in conversation. T looked embarrassed. He looked at Soulboy and could see him ask Hangers, 'Have you got any money for petrol?' and Hangers shook his head.

Soulboy drew a More from its long brown pack and lit up. He offered Hangman one.

Hangers waved his hand. 'No. Trying to give them up.'

'Good boy.'

'When are we going to do the thing?'

'When we've finished here.'

Hangers smiled. 'Are you sure it's going to be easy?'

'I'm sure.'

'Level with me. What's in it?'

'Confiscating stolen goods.'

'Who from?'

'Those two boys.'

'Didums. We might upset them. Have they got anything worth stealing? We're just doing it for a laugh, right. I don't mind screwing up the peanut again. I'm still in.'

'They've got a vanload of furs. Top quality stuff. Not so exclusive that we can't get rid of them. I've already got a buyer lined up. A man who only deals with pros. He doesn't like being let down, so he only deals with people who can deliver, like myself.'

'Nice.'

'The man's the business. He knows all the top men. He's got people that work for him who've got people who work for them and so on and so on. We're in. How does it feel to be an employer? Have someone graft for you. All we've got to do is hijack their van, leave it covered up down at Ozzy's for the night and I'll sort out the finances and stuff first thing tomorrow. I'll have to do the contract stuff alone. Trust me?'

'Any choice?'

'Not much. My man asked for it to be this way. He's a pro, man.'

'He likes to keep it cool then?'

'You know how villains with an organisation are.'

'Yes. Smart.'

'Paul can cover the van, I'm not getting my hands dirty. I'm finished with all that.'

'How did you find out what they were up to?'

'I just know, that's how. And that's enough questions. You know the score.'

'I'm still in. I'm still in. I'm with you all the way, Souls, you know that. Boy, am I going to mess him up.'

'Who?'

'That boy, Derrick.'

'You don't stand a chance.'


T fought with the viper until he vanquished it, subduing it by a gentle tease back into place.

All the while, the cashier looked out at T's battle. He

wouldn't come out of his little cubby-hole and help or open the door of the shop a wee bit to shout out some instructions on handling the machine. No, no; at this time of night he is to stay in the secured small section surrounded by toughened glass and open the door to no one. The shop is closed, done up with mortice locks and bolts. You can only get to the cashier's cubby-hole via the shop. (The shop and cashier's bit are one unit, you see.)

So, the cashier could not help Tommy even if he wanted to; which he might have, because he was smiling and appeared to be an alright guy.

Paul snored. A big broad one. Gurgly. Soulboy swivelled around on his seat in the front, drew out his hanky and flicked it in Paul's face. Smack. The hanky cracked. It stung sleepy Paul around the bottom of his nose and top lip.

Paul roused, said, 'Stop it.' So the smooth one did it again. Paul opened his eyes.

'Stop what?' Soulboy asked, taking aim with his hanky, holding it like a catapult, stretched out, using two hands and carefully sizing up the target.

*The boys would be in on the eleven forty-five. They'll ride in from out of town. And they've got long memories. There'll be a few old scores to settle. And what about the twelve just men, good and true. What's going to happen to them now? Now that the boys are coming back to town, and the sheriff's laid up sick and gonna be taken to The Bar Q ranch before they get here.*

*Those who haven't left town already are preparing for voluntary internment behind the barred doors of safe houses, or getting ready to follow the sheriff's example and go themselves. Those who stay will wait and see what happens. The boys might have changed.*

*They're here. The horsemen appear, a clippety-cloppeting through the brush on the outskirts of the settlement.*

*Gentlewomen snatch up children, call their men out of the saloon and harass the schoolmaam's father — who also runs the general store — for final bits of food. SIEGE! Only the whorehouse and saloon stay open.*

*The road is clear by the time the boys ride in. Suddenly, the town drunk stumbles out of nowhere and falls into the dust clutching his baby; a half-drunk quart. He stumbles to his feet and finds himself facing up to the boys; tall in the saddle about ten yards away.*

*'Got a dime, mister?' he feebly asks, peering through slits for eyes. One hand held out, begging, the other holding the bottle and shading his eyes from the sun.*

*The horsemen look at one another and smile. 'Dance,' one of them suggested. 'If you dance, I'll give you a dime.'*

*The old man kissed his child full on the lips and fell.*

*The dirtiest looking one, with no teeth and wearing a tatty sombrero commanded, 'Dance!' drawing his forty-five and letting it off up in the air.*

*The drunk got to his feet, all shook up. He shook so much he dropped the child.*

*Mex started shooting at his feet. 'Dance,' he kept saying as if it was the only word he knew. 'Comprendé. Levanté. Dance. Dance.'*

*The old man hopped around, evading the bullets.*

*Another one of the boys joins in. Dissatisfied he commands, 'Quicker!' And so on and so on until all the boys had a go and emptied their six-shooters. And the old man slumped to the ground, exhausted, shaking with fear, weeping like a baby and somehow appearing overall, paralysed.*

*The boys rode on. One of them dropped a dime as he rode by. The leader.*


'It hurts.'

'Shut up,' he replied, cracking Paul another stinging sharp one with the hanky. He took aim again.

'Alright, Souls.'

'Shut it.' He cracked him again. 'Shut it. Shut it. Shut it.'
And he let Paul have it three times in quick succession, then
stopped.

T Boy was at the window, on the driver's side of the car.

Hangman elbowed Paul, knocking the wind out of him. Paul
doubled up. Soulboy asked Hangman if he thought it was
necessary to elbow Paul? He then asked Paul if he was alright.
He leant over so that he could see Paul's face and patted his
back as if he was consoling a child. Paul answered Soulboy
breathlessly and crouched over embracing his ribs. 'Yes, yes.'

Soulboy turned on Hangman. 'Don't follow so close,' he said
in earnest.

'I thought you wanted me to?'

'What are you talking about?'

'Nothing. Nothing.' Hangman like a slave.

'Would I do that?'

'No. No.'

'Paul's like a brother to me.' Soulboy leant over again and
hugged Paul from a cute angle; like a don; mafia, kind of;
dead paternal.

Hangman shrunk. Unsure of how clever he was in saying
anything at all, he halfheartedly muttered, 'You're a brother,'
to Paul.

Soulboy released Paul and thumped Hangman's leg. The
stabbed leg. With clenched teeth and tight jaw, Hangers
became rigid and shook. Paul came up as Hangman went down.

'What's this, Punch and Judy? Money? For the petrol. Split it
four ways, two pounds each,' Tommy suggested, sticking his
head in.

The three guys in the car bounced blank stares off one
another. Not a murmur.

'Two pounds, Paul?' T stuck his hand through the window
and out in front of Paul's face. 'Two pounds?'

Then he moved to Hangers. 'Two?' Hangman shook his head.
T asked him again. Hangers shook his head again. T asked
him if he was alright?

Hangman shook his head, clutched his leg, groaned a bit and fell forward again. Soulboy — forever paternal — asked him if he was cool? Hangers shook his head from a huddled position.

Tommy looked at Soulboy and asked, 'What are we going to do?'

'How much have you got?' Soulboy talked like a politician.

'Two pounds. How much have you got?'

'What are we going to do?'

'You tell me?' Tommy turned and smiled at the cashier and waved.

The cashier smiled and waved back. He opened a magazine, spread it over the till and immersed himself in it.

Tom was in the car just like that, and whoosh they were off, out the forecourt and way down the road. 'Where to, Souls?'

'Drive man. It's almost picking time. The fruit should be ripe by now.'

## 22

Jenny stuck a lunchbox under his arm and sent him on his way. 'I want the box back,' she said, patting him on the back and guiding him out.

It was unexpected. 'You shouldn't have.'

'It's not much. Don't go overboard, Patrick. And I want the box back tomorrow.'

She got him out the door and was going back to the counter when he reappeared and asked if he could have a bottle of

stout as well. She went behind the bar and fetched one for
him. He sifted through some coins. She waved him away,
pointing at the door and saying, 'Go!'
'I insist,' he said, still trying to get the money together.
'Go!' she again said.
So he left, bowing and thanking her.
Pete went over and whispered in her ear, 'Not falling for him,
are you?'
'Don't be silly.'
'All women love a gentleman.'
'You should try it sometime then.'
He laughed.

## 23

Patrick was almost home. He dug into his pockets for his
keys. He searched the pocket he usually keeps them in first.
Then another and another and another. Over and over he dug
into his pockets, frantically trawling for the keys. Nothing.
He couldn't recall dropping them.
'I must have dropped them coming here,' he thought. He
began to retrace his steps, walking slowly back towards *The
Hope*. He gleaned the streets for his lost keys. 'If I don't find
them along the road they must still be in the pub somewhere,' he thought.
It started drizzling and dark clouds loomed way at the base
of the earth. The backdrop-cum-sky was painted blue with
white blotches — up above — moving along to splodges and

estuaries of red then darker and darker until black. The darkness crept closer and closer and would soon be overhead, crying on all of them. Patrick made himself snug and carried on his way smartly. He upturned his jacket collar and held his lapels — turned inward — together a little below his throat. The lunchbox was squeezed tightly under his arm. His wet clothes went limp and hung about him like robes. A plimsoll squelched as he walked.

Something shiny glinted from beside the wheel of a car on the opposite side of the road. It caught his eye and he made a bee-line for it. The squelching plimsolled foot landed in a small pool of rainwater which had burst the banks of the gutter at the side of the pavement. It began to sound like a flat raspberry. But Patrick didn't pay any attention. His eyes were focussed on the shiny object, which turned out to be a silver toy soldier; rifle with fixed bayonet, uniformed and looking dead serious.

The discomfort at once dawned on him. So he leisurely sat on a low wall, took off his shoe and tipped the water out like a man without a worry in the world. With care and attention he lifted the shoe and angled it so the water would spill out slowly and in a steady controlled stream. He completed the outpouring by letting droplets fall one after the other, at timed precise intervals. When he'd drained the shoe he smiled with satisfaction.

'Home again,' thought Patrick, as the proverbial fish taking to water but more literal than that. He opened the lunchbox, tilting the lid so it acted as a cowl and prevented his food getting wet. Jenny'd packed a nice piece of chicken. It was right in the middle, surrounded by sandwiches and biscuits separated by napkins. He moved to the wall a few houses down from where he was. Two big trees sheltered part of the wall and made a good impromptu restaurant. He held the chicken with a napkin, to keep his fingers clean and took big rapid bites. Finished, and oil and strands of chicken cover his face but his fingers are still clean. He wiped his face with a napkin, took the bottle of stout from his pocket, unscrewed it, took a healthy swig and belched like he meant it.

Crack! A streak of lightning. Now you see me now you don't. Vibrant, loud and the centre of attention for that split second, then gone. Without warning it came and whipped across the sky. Now the thunder rolls. Too late to serve warning of its master's coming. It rained heavily for a short time, gradually subsiding until it ceased. And you could see the backdrop shift as the clouds changed formation up above and far ahead. The dark clouds that were above moved on and up above was now reddy-blue. Threatening fresh dark clouds loomed beyond them, so more of the same could be expected. Tonight the sky envelops the world. The buildings and monuments fall into the backcloth, like grey inanimate pillars in one way, like cardboard cut-outs in another, but insignificant for sure.

While the rain bucketed down, Patrick dried out in his little enclave eating sandwiches and drinking beer. He closed the box, shoved the part-drunk bottle in his pocket, stood up, stretched and set about finding his keys. Then he remembered dropping them outside the pub earlier on. The pub is where he'd have ended up anyway, so he carried on in the same direction, still squelching and not completely dried out. At least he needn't dawdle now. All he has to do is get there. There's no need to be on the look-out for anything. It's simply a matter of head down and get moving.

A car came up behind him. At a fair speed at first, then slower and more ominous as Patrick — head down — made his way back.

# Sticks and Stones

## 24

The pub seldom closes at the right time. It's a job and a half to get everyone to drink up and leave by eleven. The last person's usually out by quarter or twenty past; to join the couples and cliques who'll hang around the courtyard until say eleven thirty, when a few couples — arm in arm — walk off into the night and groups get into cars, slamming the doors so that the crowd will look over and see the gleaming transporter. By eleven thirty-five, the courtyard's empty.

Biggre and D stumbled out, drunk as lords. Biggre had his arm slung over his closest pal. And what was he wearing? The black polo-neck and cords for a second time. He's slipping.
'Shall we drive?' Biggre asked suggestively.
'We're not going to use the estate again. It's dumped, let it stay.'
'We'll get something nice and cruise.'
'Yeah. Let's cruise.' They tripped and tumbled and bumbled their way as far as the yard wall and fell against it. 'Still want to drive?' D asked.
'Don't know.'
'Want to die?'
'No. Definitely no.'
'You don't want to drive then, do you?'
'Don't think so, no.'
'How are we going to get past this wall?'
Biggre stared through it. 'What wall?'
'Come off it, Biggre.'

'Don't know.' He added sensationally, 'It's been raining,' and propped his arm over the top of the wall for support. Derrick had let himself go. His weight was being borne more and more by Biggre's other arm, which was still over Derrick's shoulder. Biggre summed up, 'I can't drive. You can't stand up, let alone walk. We're a great team.'

'I think I'm going to be sick.'

'Put your head over the wall.'

D inanimate, moaned and retched, though nothing came up.

'Put your head over.' Biggre turned him around and held his head down over the wall. 'You do need your mummy, don't you?'

Derrick heaved and bursts of vomit cascaded out over the pavement. He pushed Biggre's hand away and brought his head up for an instant, to tell Biggre not to push his luck. He then heaved again and had to get his head back down.

'It's always there, isn't it? Just under the surface, it's always there.'

'And what's that? What's under the surface?'

'Who knows? It's none of my business. You're too touchy.'

'I feel better now.'

'When you feel like you're going to be sick, there's no point holding back, it's best to let it all out. You always feel better afterwards. I'm not feeling too bad myself now, for just a little cooling out in the fresh air.'

'Yeah.' D slung his arm around Biggre. Biggre gave him a wary glance.

'Who cares?' D asked, sitting down in the wet and leaning against the wall.

Biggre sat beside him. Derrick reslung his arm around his matey. Biggre put his hand in one of his pockets and flushed out a half-smoked draw. He lit up. 'Want some?'

'No.'

Biggre smoked, staring up into the ever-changing sky. The yard was clear and the night quiet. It was like the whole upper sphere moved around them in a soothing yet foreboding way. 'It's better than drink.'

'I'm not really a drinker.'

'Obviously. I'm not into it much either.'

'I didn't hear you refusing any.'

'Stick around. You'll have plenty of other opportunities. You'll never see me booze again.'

'That doesn't explain tonight. Why drink today? Why not yesterday? Last year? Next year?'

'The vibe was right. It carried me.'

'That's funny talk.'

'Don't complain, you need the company.'

'I don't need anyone.'

'Not even a woman?'

'I've got a woman.'

'Her name?'

'Naomi.'

'Nice name. I've never seen you with her.'

'Do you see me twenty-four hours a day, every day?'

'No. But I've never seen you with any woman.'

'Don't get funny.'

'I'm not being funny. Let's go to a club, hunt down two sisters.'

'There's no certainty we'll get anything. Only makes things worse if you draw a blank.'

'Impossible!'

'It's not impossible.'

'Okay then, let's go to one of them massage places. We'll have the house speciality.'

'Waste of money.'

'You've never had the house speciality. You'll still have a hundred left after the full treatment. That's plenty nuff.'

'How do you know so much? Pervert. Anyway, I thought you didn't like whores.'

'I didn't say that.'

'Joanne,' D prompted.

'What?'

'This afternoon. By the wall. Here.'

'Oh, the white girl. I like her. She's got spirit.'

'You like her?'

'Yes, yes, but she's not for me. The vibe isn't right.'

'I sort of got the impression that something was wrong. I thought you wanted to kill her?'

'No way. I like her. You know how it is sometimes. I don't know what got into me. Believe me. I just don't know. I could have hurt her. She spared me.'

In unbelief Derrick reiterated, 'She spared you,' and paused.

'Why do you call her a whore and all that rubbish?'

'Does your woman work?'

A speechless Derrick.

'What does she do? You think a lot of her, don't you? I mean, you think about her a lot and like her too. Both ways.'

'My bag.'

'You left it in the car.'

D jumped up. 'I've got to go and get it. I've got to go and get it.'

'How are you going to get in the car? Can you pick a lock?'

'I'll smash it.'

'Cool down, man. Whatever's in the bag, you don't need.'

'Don't tell me what I need.'

'You'll get caught. You know it's not smart to go anywhere near that car again. You said so yourself.'

A cop car shot past, going like the clappers. A packed police van whizzed behind the car by a few seconds. Biggre and Derrick looked at one another. Derrick sat down.

'You don't need it, D.'

'No. I guess I don't. What's the trick with the gear?'

'No trick. The clothes maketh the man. What you wear is what you are.'

'Bullshit. What's the trick? What do you do? Stash things at strategic points, carry the stuff in a bag, wear two or three trousers and shirts; you must get hot. How do you do it?'

'So, it's Naomi is it? Whereabouts does she live?'

'That's enough!'

'Touchy about her, aren't you? Then again, you're touchy about almost everything.'

'That's right, like you.'

'I'm not touchy.'

'What are you then?'

'Naomi's brother.'

'Never.'

Biggre winked.

'You don't look like her. I didn't know she had any brothers?'

'Don't know much about her do you?'

'I know all that matters.'

'Do you think so?'

'Look, man, just leave it. She's none of your affair.'

'I'm her brother. I can say what I like about her.'

'Maybe you can say what you like about her, that doesn't mean you can say it to me.' They sat in silence for a bit. 'Hold on. You're not her brother.' Derrick thought back to school days. 'She never even noticed you on the way home from school.'

'What do you mean? You didn't know me at school. When I left, you were in the first year.'

'No. Second. And who didn't know you at school. You had the biggest mouth in the whole place. You guys used to try and check all the girls. Who could miss you?'

'So I have seen her.'

'Don't mess!'

'Keep calm. I'm just joking.'

'A joke can cost you your life.'

'Whew.'

'Don't mess.'

'Okay, okay. Still want to cruise?'

'In what?'

'I told you. We'll pick something up. Something nice. You don't fancy the massage parlour?'

'I don't know.'

'It'll help you loosen up.'

'Let me think about it,' Derrick replied, getting to his feet. 'I wish I had my tools.'

'You don't need them, I tell you.'

'I'm not so sure.'

Biggre got up too and he and Derrick walked off together.

'Ever jukked anybody?'

'What are you asking me?'

'Simple enough question. Have you ever jukked someone? Yes or no?'

'I don't know.'

'What do you mean, you don't know.'

'I've thought about it.'

'Thinking about it's the difference between whole and punctured lungs. In the time it takes you to think about it, a real bad man could take your piece and use it on you.'

'Move from me, man!' D turned around and walked away from Biggre.

Biggre called after him but D just kept going. Biggre disappeared.

## 25

And reappeared from the red estate with the bag in his hand. Derrick sucked his teeth, walked straight up to Biggre and snatched the bag, nearly dropping it. They chuckled together.

D told Biggre that he'd have managed without any help. The

bag seemed to have got a lot heavier. He slung it over his shoulder. 'I'm tired.'

'Are you going up to your friend's.'

'No. I think I'll go home.'

'We'll pick up a car. I'll drive you.'

'Where? Up the wall. Let's cruise.'

'Now you're talking.'

'I feel alright now that I've got this.' He patted the bag.

'Feel secure?'

'All my security's right here. In this little holdall.'

'Looks like that little holdall has got hold of you.'

'Let's quit the conversation and just walk. Keep things friendly.'

'Your wish is my command.'

'Make me rich and happy.'

'Done. We'll get a porsche or something.'

'A jag. I've always liked jags.'

'No problem.'

They carried on in silence, unconsciously marching in time. Their steps had a beat like, slap ffsssh, slap ffsssh, slap; like a tom-tom and hi-hat beat consecutively. Biggre passed intermittent comments about this and that but Derrick didn't respond; not by nodding his head or showing any change in the focus of his attention or anything. He'd travelled to his own private planet. Biggre could see he was somewhere else and left him there. He could have shouted or prodded him into being more attentive to life on earth, but he didn't.

Derrick's planet was inhabited by two people only; himself and Naomi. He could visualise the two of them, together, his head in her lap. She, running her fingers over and through his hair, toying with his ears, kissing his lips and saying, 'It's alright now. It's all over. You're with me now. You're not going to get caught. I'll protect you. I understand how you feel. They deserved it. Any man worth his salt would have done it.' Thereby making him feel calm. He decided to see her this very night. He saw himself striding up to her door and being fobbed off with excuses by her mother or father or both. He'd insist and they'd urge him to leave their door, become frustrated at his insistence and stubbornness and slam the door in his face. 'Which was what they wanted to do all the time,' he'd say to himself. So he'd kick down the door, barge in and tell Naomi to come. As if under a spell, she'd follow him slavishly. Her father would plead with her not to go, her mother would scream and twirl around like a frenzied dervish; all to no avail as Naomi adoringly parades behind her champion. Derrick foresaw all this clearly, but it could only happen if done this night. After tonight she would be his forever.

'What about a BM?' Biggre prodded Derrick with his elbow.

'What?'

'A BM. Over there.' He pointed at a black BMW parked down the road.

'It'll do. Do you know T Boy and Hangers?'

'Doesn't everybody?'

'Where can I find them?'

'What do you want with them?'

'Personal business. Where!'

'I don't know. What do you want with them?'

'I don't want all of them, just one.'

'Which one?'

'Hangman.'

'You're crazy.'

Derrick punched Biggre on the side of his head and he fell. 'Don't call me crazy.'


'Scavengers. Scavengers.' It was Paul, pointing — as is his wont — at them and laughing. All four in the car wore anxious, expectant smiles.

## 26

Hangman drew his piece out from under the seat and flew out the car, to stand not more than a couple of paces from D and the fallen wizard. 'Say your prayers, boy.'

Soulboy said, 'Idiot. I bet he doesn't use it. Let's collect,' and got out the car too.

Tommy Boy turned on the beam and it shot forward, capturing Patrick; putting him in the spotlight, centre stage. T called him and he seized up.

Paul came out cackling, gleefully clutching a small bundle of cloth.

'Hey, Hangers, cool down. I want to talk to the man. I believe we have a little business to discuss. You can have him after me,' said Soulboy.

Hangman winked at Derrick. 'Later.' He smiled insipidly and turned his back on D in a nonchalant way.

D just said 'Fuck you' and dipped into his bag for a tool to complete his day in the only fashion it could be completed. The mallet and blade and axe had gone. 'Bricks,' he thought as he groped urgently. 'Oh what the hell.' He dragged up a half-brick and set to work on the back of Hangman's head.

Hangman slumped prone to the ground. He dropped the sword. He slithered away smartly like a snake; crawling along the muddy road to Soulboy's shoes and safety. Soulboy kicked Hangman in the face and said, 'Move!' Hangman withered away whimpering.

'You want some?' D asked.

'I want more than that, boy,' Soulboy replied. 'Fisticuffs is dirty stuff. I want the goodies.' A hanky ghosted into his hands and he wiped them busily and patted his lips with it. 'The furs.'

T Boy shepherded and shifted Patrick over. 'That's right. That's right. Over here. No, not there. Over here. That's right. At last. Stay right there. I should have been a director. Now, doesn't that look nice. Two little scavengers all in a row.' He

snatched the lunchbox from Patrick. 'What's this, din-dins?'
and tossed it frisbee-like over and beyond the car.

Paul giggled.

'Remember me? You put your dog on me. That's not a
friendly thing to do. I bet you wish you were my friend now.
Shame,' Soulboy said.

Paul looked at Hangman, drooping at his side. 'Don't come
on like we're spars.' Paul slapped him. 'Move!' Hangman
drifted off the scene lifelessly. 'Move!' Paul again barked.
Then Hangman all but disappeared. (Only one person can
truly disappear like magic.)

Soulboy watched Hangman walk. 'Knew it.' He paused and
became overtly thoughtful, every so often he'd throw a
pleasant glance at D. It was a funny glance. Not quite on
the level. A glance hard to describe. Sort of paternal. A look
of approval. A glance to make D think Soulboy thought
him worthy. 'Hey, I'll tell you what. To save all the aggra-
vation, you can come in with us and we'll split the winnings.
I always knew you'd do Hangers. You can have the wanker's
share.'

D looked for Biggre but he'd gone. 'Shit,' he thought.

'You're not talking to me. Don't you like me? I'm Soulboy.
A nice guy. The number one man. Show me where the furs
are, we'll flog them and split the readies. Can I be fairer than
that. Butch is cheap, forget him, if that's what's worrying
you. I've got all the angles. Everything's worked out.'

'I haven't got any furs!' Derrick answered, real crisp.

T punched an unsuspecting Patrick in the stomach. 'You've
got to learn to come when I say come.'

Patrick rocked but didn't fall and wasn't winded. T staring at
Patrick, stepped back from him tentatively. He could tell he
hadn't hurt his captive to the extent he'd intended. His captive
knew it too. They exchanged the quality of their eye to eye
confrontations. The captive's stare gained the initiative and
threatened, and Tommy's became apprehensive.

Soulboy took up Hangman's cane. 'You've had a bit of luck,

now don't push it. Tell me where the stuff is and let's all be friends.'

'Look. I said there are no furs,' Derrick reaffirmed.

'I know you did the warehouse tonight.'

'What warehouse? It was a factory and it was empty.'

'Empty?' Soulboy chuckled. 'You're a comedian. Very funny.' He clapped. Paul clapped too. 'Where are they? Come on.' He began to draw the blade. 'Come on! Come on!'

Derrick hauled up a brick and set himself up to move and strike and move and strike and move 'cos he wasn't going down without taking one of them with him.

Soulboy sheathed the sword, walked back to the car and slid the sabre back under the seat. 'Paul,' he called out.

'Okay.' Paul unravelled the cloth to reveal a thirty-eight.

Tommy saw Paul with the gun. 'You never told me anything about this. Souls, what are you doing giving that fool a gun? Guns, man? They'll lock us up and throw away the key if they catch us packing. Put the fucking thing away, Paul. Hey, Souls, the guy says he hasn't got the stuff. Let's leave it at that. There's going to be other jobs.'

'Shoot him, Paul.'

As ordered, Paul sized Tommy up.

'Alright, Souls. Alright.' T backed off from the bad guys until he was standing in line with Patrick and D. And then there were three.

D stared straight at Paul. 'Fuck off. You aint going to use it.' Paul giggled and took aim at him.

'Where is my merchandise?' Soulboy asked.

'No merchandise,' D replied.

Souls floated up to Derrick and softly said, 'I don't believe you.' He flashed his hand by D's shoulder and slit his jacket, shirt and arm ever so slightly. D bled and spat on the ground. Soulboy wafted away from D; back to where he'd floated in from. 'See what I mean. I'm a pro. That's the difference between me and you guys. I'm an expert.' He sniffed a perfumed hanky and wiped his hands.

All in black,
coming round the back
of the bad boys car,
Biggre. Tommy, Patrick and D could see him. Tommy didn't
call out. Biggre spun his forearms around in a hula hoop
fashion and pointed at his mouth and ducked behind the car
and appeared again, giving the sign again. He did it a few
times before Patrick caught on; keep talking. 'What do I get
out of this?' Patrick asked.

'You? You get cut to cubes if you don't shut it. That's what
you get,' Soulboy laughed. Paul didn't, he looked shivery and
waved the gun along the line up, staring at the boys through
terrified eyes.

'Your man's falling apart,' D suggested.

'So what. I don't need anyone but me, and that's your
problem if you get what I mean.'

'Hey, Souls, let's forget it. Can't you see there's something
wrong about this? It's not our style. It aint smooth.'

'Shut it, T. I don't know you anymore.'

'Isn't this going too far?'

'Don't push, man. Don't push.'

'Alright, Souls.'

'Just to show that I'm a reasonable man, if you say there's no
furs, there's no furs. I'll take your word for it. I believe you. I
can't be any more reasonable than that now, can I? I'll take
everything else you've got.'

'What?' Tommy Boy, like in a state of shock.

'Everything. Your money. Your rings. Your clothes. Everything.'

'Underpants?'

'Everything.'

Derrick squared up to him. 'Get lost.'

'Everything, I said. Unless you want to play with my man
and his cannon.'

'Who says that gun's real anyway. It could be a dummy. That
would be right up your street. Another dummy. Like your
ace bouncer, Hangman.'

112

'You think I'm into playing kiddies games? Is that what you think? You think I'm like that idiot? Don't you know I'm the real stuff? I'll show you. I'll show you I don't mess around.' He patted his face furiously with a hanky. He kept his eyes on the guys in front. Paul flapped about behind him. Souls perspired. He became bitter and sharp but tried to keep looking good. Without turning he ordered, 'Show them, Paul. Show them.'

'Paul's asleep,' came the reply.

Soulboy spun round fast. 'You?'

'Yes me. Biggre.'

'Where's Paul?'

Biggre nodded at the car. Paul was sprawled across the back seat, his legs stuck out of the rear door. Biggre made a karate chopping motion at his own neck to show Soulboy how it was done. He'll be alright. He's asleep, that's all.'

'Fuck him.'

'And I thought you were friends.'

'I don't need friends and I don't need an army to handle you.'

'He's a pro, Biggre,' T Boy said. 'Shouldn't you shiver?'

'Yeah. A real pro. Real gun and all. Shame he didn't have any bullets. Bullets maketh the gun,' Biggre added for good measure.

'Hey, Tommy, you don't want to fool around with me.'

'You terrify me, Souls. Terrify me. Can't you see the whole thing's screwed up?'

'Screwed up?' Soulboy shrieked and drew his personal blade; the one you never see. 'Me and you, Tommy. Me and you.'

Tommy snatched the brick out of Derrick's hand and hurtled it into the sweet one's face, then bundled him to the floor before he had a chance to use the blade. He kicked the knife from his friend's palm, then again, further and out of reach. 'Paul would kill himself with that gun you gave him before he kills someone else. Paul is dangerous to himself.'

'I'm dangerous all the time and that's the way it's going to stay. I'm especially dangerous for you. From now on that's the way it's going to be. You'd better watch out. I'm going to be bad for your health. Think about it!'

'Do you want me to beat your brains out, here and now?'

'Do it then. Do it! Do it! You're fuck all. You haven't got what it takes.'

Derrick walked up and kicked Soulboy in the nuts. 'Why waste your breath on him?' he asked Tommy. He looked down on Soulboy. 'Cool off!'

Soulboy groaned. 'Alright, alright, alright.'

'Help me get him up.'

Derrick and Tommy Boy dragged Soulboy to the back seat of the BMW and slung him down, over Paul. They shoved the two pairs of feet inside and closed the door.

Tommy looked at D, Biggre and Patrick and said 'Cool' meaning, we have a long way to go and the next time we meet, if we meet, we'll have respect for each other and maybe he meant sorry.

Biggre said 'Cool' in agreement or acceptance and D did the same. Patrick said, 'See you in the pub sometime.'

'Okay,' T replied and got into the car and drove off with the crew.

Butch and Joanne drew up in a cab.

## 27

Joanne refused to get out of the cab. 'It would be different if he wasn't here,' she explained. 'I couldn't go through all that rubbish twice in one day. What's Derrick having a go at him about?'

'I don't know.' Butch asked the cab driver to wait. 'Two minutes.'

'A quid for every half hour waiting time. That's the rate, mate,' the cab driver replied.

'It's covered.'

'It's your money. And I only carry four passengers.'

'Who said there'd be any more passengers?'

'Just letting you know, mate.'

Butch kissed his teeth. 'I'll be back in a minute,' he said to Jo. He got out of the cab and made his way over to the victorious triumvirate.

Patrick collected his lunchbox and resumed his mission. Butch passed him as he moved away from the other two. 'What are you doing around here?' he asked.

'What are you, a police man,' Patrick replied. 'Where were you when your friends needed you?'

Butch wanted to ask him what he meant but didn't get the chance, as Patrick simply made his statement and walked on by, with his chest puffed out, full of confidence and well-cocky; cocky enough to have the final word and go. Away, the seaman, the buccaneer, the fearless adventurer, like Errol Flynn, so smooth, so heroic.


Biggre prodded his thumb at Butch. 'Here comes your minder,' he said to D.

'No, Biggre. I thought you were my minder,' D replied.

'You should be grateful.'

'Grateful for what. You could have got me killed. You're a pain in the arse.'

They almost laughed.

Butch butted in. 'What's going on here? You'd better watch yourself, D.' He pointed at the bag. 'Still walking around with that load of trouble?'

'Yeah,' D replied. 'More trouble than you could imagine. What are you doing here anyway? You haven't come out to check up on me have you?'

'Someone's got to look out for you.'

'Well I have good news for you, Butch. Your worries are over. You have an assistant. An able ally; Biggre.' Derrick slung an arm over Biggre's shoulder. They jostled one another. Biggre, pretending to push D away and D, pretending to try and trip Biggre up. They mucked around like schoolboys in a playground.

'What's going on?'

D picked up the bag and emptied the bricks out onto the ground.

Butch scratched his head. 'Where are the hammers and stuff?'

'That's a point, Biggre, where are they?'

'At the bottom of the canal, where they can't do any harm. Weighted down with some rocks. You didn't need them.'

'He didn't need them?' Butch asked.

'We messed them up, Butch. Remember that lesson they needed, we gave it to them. They tried to roll us. Hangman's nothing, Butch. Nothing. Is that cab waiting for you? Is it who I think it is in the back? Want to give me a lift?'

'Where to?'

'Ten minutes away.'

'Okay.'

'Coming, Biggre?' Biggre had gone; left this sphere; in a puff of smoke the master of multifarious modes made off. 'How does he do that, Butch?'

'Search me. Have you got a passport?'

'Yes. Somewhere. I haven't seen it since I went on school holidays.'

'You went on school holidays?'

'Yes, Italy. Venice. On the gondolas and everything. Have you got one?'

'Of course. I never thought I'd ever use it though.'

'Where are we going?'

'LA.'

'How?'

'Joanne.'

116

'Piss off.'

'I'm on the level. We're going, man. Joanne'll sort out two of the tickets. If we put our money together, we can get hold of a third one.'

'I'll check her out myself.'

'She's okay, D.'

They got into the cab. 'Where to?' the cabbie asked.

Derrick told him the address.

'That's up my way,' Joanne said. 'Who do you know around there? Is it a woman? I might know her. It's a bit late to call round isn't it? You must know her pretty well.'

'Shut up!' Derrick prepared himself for installing the final piece of the jigsaw into place.


## 28

Derrick asked the cabbie if he had space for another person.

'Four's my maximum, mate,' he answered.

'That's four excluding himself,' Butch added. 'It's alright. Who are you bringing? Is it her, D?'

'I've got to, Butch. I can't make the move without her.'

'Are you sure?'

'What's one hundred per cent?'

'Why can't you settle for seventy-five, like everyone else?'

'Another time, Butch. Another time.'

They came to the road. It was tree lined and wide with wide double-bayed houses and much like Derrick's road with the exception of D's road having single-bayed homes.

'Whereabouts, mate?'

'On the left. Down there, behind the Volvo Estate,' D replied.

'I suppose you want me to wait again?'

Butch got irate. 'So what. You'll get your money.'

'The rate's a quid every half hour, waiting time.'

'You've already said that.'

'Just thought your mate ought to know, mate.'

'How much is it?' Butch asked.

The cab driver gave the meter a quick look and ran through some swift mental arithmetic. 'Four fifty, mate.'

'Stop the car.'

'Where? Here?'

'Yes, stop the car!'

Derrick sprang out without prompting. 'Let's go,' Butch said to Joanne. She followed him. Butch slung a fiver on the back seat. 'Be lucky, mate.'

'What about your change?'

'Have a drink on me.'

'Thanks, mate.'

'Arsenic,' Butch suggested under his breath. The cab pulled away.

Derrick was making his way up the steps of a house about twenty yards away from where the cab had stopped.

'This girl called Naomi lives there,' Joanne said. 'Are they related? Does he know her family? Real snobs. A bit late to call round, isn't it?'

'You know her?'

'Who? Naomi? Of course. I thought she was going out with some bloke, studying law or something. What's Derrick doing with her? Her mum and dad wouldn't like him.'

'Shit!'

'Does he want to bring her? No chance! And he calls me crazy!'

Derrick rang the doorbell, hammered at the door and yelled her name through the letterbox, 'Naomi. Naomi.' The lights came on next door.

'Derrick, you're waking up the whole street. They're not in. Let's split.'

'Yeah, Derrick. LA, a new start. What are you waiting for, come on.' Butch and Joanne started up the steps after him.

'Get back, Butch,' Derrick barked. Butch and Jo retreated from the steps to the pavement. 'They're here!'

Butch persisted. 'If they are, it doesn't look as if they're going to open up for you.'

'They'll open up alright.' D barged the door. 'Naomi, open this fucking door.'

Joanne to Butch. 'Your mate's so subtle.'

'Why's everyone on his back? He's my spar, alright. Now get off.'

'Sorry, Butch.'

'Don't be sorry, just get off his back and stay off, alright.'

'Alright, Butch. Alright. But he's not going the right way about this.'

'Is there a right way?'

'I don't think so. I think he's wasting his time. And I always thought he was the smart one out of you two.'

'He's alright.'

A middle-aged woman came out of the house next door and asked what was going on. Derrick stared hard at her with those red eyes and didn't say a word. The woman became a bit anxious and seemed to be edging back through the door. Derrick's stare unsettled her. She probably mistook it for the stare of a crazed thing, but no, we know D, it was puppy dog helplessness and frustration that made his eyes red. He wanted to bawl. If the woman went up close and peered straight into his eyes the tears would have been unmistakable. The woman turned to Butch and Joanne. 'There's nobody in,' she said.

Joanne responded. 'Okay. Thanks.'

'She aint there, Derrick. Let's split.'

The woman went back inside her house. Derrick gave the door two huge kicks and slowly dragged himself away.

Joanne gave D a consoling little hug. 'It's probably all for the best, Del.'

'Shut up, woman.' He pushed her away.

'Aren't you finished yet?' Butch asked.

'I want her.'

'What if you can't have her?'

A neat sports car passed them as they walked away from Naomi's. It parked behind the Volvo. Naomi and the curly permed boy got out.

'She's mine, Butch,' Derrick turned back.

'Stay here, Joanne,' Butch followed him.


*She couldn't spend another moment in the small town. 'Small town full of big dicks,' she'd say. 'Men who go to church and pay their tithes on Sunday and give her juke box and pepsi money for two minutes inside her pussy the other six days of the week; sometimes even Sunday night.'*

*'Peanuts and piss,' she thought. 'There's a life out there, better than this.'*

*It's all gonna be different now she's with Billy Ray and Willy Good Eye. Those boys have ideas. She's leaving with them tonight. They're going to collect her in their automobile. They've just got to do a little more fixing on it and it'll go faster than the sheriff's. Sure as hell, they're gonna try and track her down. Shit, which town wants to lose its only piece of young skirt. She sympathised with them.*

*Willy's got a tommy-gun and Billy Ray's got a pistol and they're fixing on making some easy dough and wasting anybody who gets in their way. The fat stinking sheriff included. She thought back to the time he caught her behind the barn with the dude from upstate. He fined the man a hundred on the spot and threatened him so much he ran off forgetting his shorts. Then the sheriff made her suck him off. 'You'd better keep buttoned up about this,' he said with his flies undone. He stunk like he'd never seen water. She smelt shit. She hoped the sheriff would chase them all on his own. He wouldn't stand a chance against the boys. They'd shoot his balls off. His fat stinking balls.*

*She dreamt of satin sheets, fancy clothes, fast cars and anything but this small cotton-picking nothing of a place. And it's gonna happen tonight when she steals away.*

*Their ascent from small town dirt farmers to American heroes will make worthy reading. Yeah, The Ballad of Billy Ray, Willy and Me.*

## 29

'Naomi,' Derrick shouted.

'What do you want?'

'I want to talk to you. I rang you at work. Didn't you get my message? I'll kill that supervisor. I told her it was important.'

'You know you're not supposed to ring me at work.'

'Do you want to talk to this guy?' Old Straight Head chimed in.

'Fuck off,' Butch replied.

Derrick turned round from facing Naomi and grinned at his mate. His grin said, 'Well, well, I'm surprised.'

'It's alright. Go on in. I'll be along in a minute. These are old friends.'

'Okay. If you're sure. What are you doing with these weirdos?'

'It's alright. Go on.' She slung him her keys. He went up the steps and opened the front door with the keys she gave him. He left the front door wide open.

'Who's that?' D asked.

'A friend,' she replied.

'A friend? It looks like it. I thought you couldn't stand him and his mates?'

'Look, I have to get on with them. I work with them, you know.'

'Yeah, you might have to get on with them. But what are you doing now? Getting it on with him?'

Butch walked away, back to Jo. Jo smiled as he strode up to her. She said quietly, 'My man.' Butch couldn't hear her. All he was concerned with was how sexy she looked. A much different girl from the one waiting for a friend by the pub wall this afternoon.


'What do you want, Derrick? Can't it wait? This is so embarrassing.'

'Come to the States with me?'

'Come to the States with you?'

'Yes. That's what I said.'

'Are you alright, Derrick? You don't even look well. What's happening to you? Look at these people you hang out with.'

'Are you coming?'

'I can't leave just like that. I've got a career and a family.'

'And a man.'

'Let's leave it. Ring me tomorrow. Derrick, we'll talk about this.' She turned away from him.

He spat on the ground and grabbed her by the arm. 'Don't turn your back on me. Is that guy your man?'

'Don't be stupid. What are you, crazy?'

'Is he your man? Yes or no?'

'Let me go, Derrick.'

'Is he? Give me a straight fucking answer.'

'Use your imagination, Derrick. And let go of my arm.' She threw a dirty look at the hand he held her with and noticed the blood stains on his jacket sleeve. 'What have you done?'

'Whatever I've done, it's been for you. I've always loved you, Naomi. But I need you, now.' His passion became greater with each syllable. It strides over skyscrapers, soars over the mountains, flew with the eagle and mingled with the stars. His impassioned arms reach out to embrace her, then press her closer and closer until clay-like, they mesh and mould into one.

She slips away and his passion subsides. There's an audible hush that seems to last an eternity. D pushed his hands out to her palms up, pleading wordlessly.

'Don't touch me. Don't touch me. Don't touch me.'

'It was for you. I had to do it for you. Can't you see? Don't you understand?'

'Yes, I can see. And I understand all I need to. Oh, my God.'

D grasped her hair and flashed his money in front of her face. 'Here is freedom. Our freedom. Now we can go anywhere, do anything. Nobody asks any questions or tells you what to do, when you're free.'

'How much is that? Fifty pounds. It's nothing. Let me go. I don't want it. I don't want anything to do with it.'

'LA?'

'For fucksake let me go, Derrick. Let me go.'

'LA?'

'Derrick, please let me go. Please.'

'I need you, Naomi.' He pushed her away; not far; not too hard. Staring at him, she immediately screams. He hits her across her head, once, and she falls to the ground. He stands above her for an instant before falling to his knees beside her and again shoving the money in front of her face. 'I need you.'


'Butch, Butch,' Joanne shouted pointing at Derrick and the woman. Derrick was coming on like a preacher caught by the spirit offering salvation. Naomi's man ran out into the street brandishing a carving knife. He kicked Derrick in the head. D keeled over, blood trickled from the corner of his mouth and his body quivered.

Butch ran up to the straight head as he was helping Naomi to her feet. He waved the knife at Butch threateningly and moved up the stairs and indoors with his girlfriend.

## 30

Joanne cradled D's head in her lap.
'Is he alright?' Butch asked.
'Yes. He's alright.' She continued softly, 'I think he's just upset.'
'Well, at least now he knows he aint Clint Eastwood.'
'I made a mistake, I'm sorry. I made a mistake,' Derrick murmured.
Life isn't like the movies.